"At every chance you hit out at me."

Verity replied cautiously to Ramón's accusation. "You could say I make the most of my opportunities."

"We're two of a kind, then," Ramón told her, so close that his tangy after-shave assailed her senses. "I take advantage of my opportunities, too."

Before she could protest he'd claimed her lips, fanning a spark of pleasure into a flame that threatened to consume her. All Verity wanted was for the embrace to continue forever....

But when Ramón finally released her, his eyes held a glint of satisfaction, and she cursed herself for succumbing so easily. What must he think of her?

The answer was painfully obvious. "What a shame we need words to communicate, Verity," he said softly, faintly mocking. "We get along so much better using other methods...."

The Overlord

by

SUSANNA FIRTH

Harlequin Books

TORONTO • LONDON • LOS ANGELES • AMSTERDAM
SYDNEY • HAMBURG • PARIS • STOCKHOLM • ATHENS • TOKYO

Original hardcover edition published in 1982
by Mills & Boon Limited

ISBN 0-373-02493-2

Harlequin Romance first edition August 1982

CHAPTER ONE

'DAD, I want to talk to you.'

Verity poured herself some more strong black coffee and sat cradling the cup in her hands, wondering how best to broach what was on her mind. She had tried various oblique approaches to the subject in the last few days, but none of them had got her very far. Perhaps it was time for some plain speaking.

She looked across the dinner table to where her father sat, his plate pushed aside, absorbed in reading a letter. They were lucky at Vista Hermosa to receive a daily delivery, unlike the more remote *estancias* which had to rely on a twice-weekly service unless someone was going into town, but her father left the house at sun-up and was often not back until late, and the evening ritual of opening the mail was a tradition that was one of her earliest childhood memories.

'Dad?' she repeated anxiously.

Mark Williams looked up at that. 'Sorry, love, I'm neglecting you. I suppose I've been on my own for so long now that I've become rather anti-social in my habits. It's too late to reform me, I think.' He smiled ruefully at her. 'Your first trip home in quite a while and your only relative totally ignores you! Will I ever be forgiven?'

'Don't be silly.' Verity gave him an affectionate glance. 'I know you're busy. When aren't you?'

'You must be very bored here on your own all day, and I'm not the most scintillating of companions in the evening, am I? Would you like to change your mind about that invitation you had to stay with your old school friend in Cordoba? I expect I could spare someone to drive you there. I can't let you drive yourself—I need the car at this end—but——'

'No, Dad.'

'That sounded very definite.'

'It was meant to be.' She played nervously with her coffee spoon, then let it drop with a clatter again. 'I'm not a child that needs amusing every moment of the day. In fact, I'm not a child at all. I'm grown up now.'

'All of eighteen.'

'Nineteen next month,' she corrected him.

'Nearly ready for drawing your old age pension!'

'Don't tease me, Dad. I'm trying to be serious.'

'About what? There's no need to be bothering your head about anything—even at what you consider to be a ripe old age. You haven't a scrap to worry about.'

'Haven't I?' She spoke sharply.

He frowned. 'What do you mean? If it's university you're on about, I thought that was all settled. We agreed that you wouldn't go to England until next year. There's plenty of time for all that, and you know how I'd worry about you on your own in London. Another year will let you do a bit of growing up, learn about life. I was sixteen when I left home for Argentina and, believe me, I know how tough it is starting again in a strange country, whether you've friends there or not.'

'No, it's not that,' she told him.

'Then what?'

'Dad, there's something wrong, isn't there?' Well, it was out in the open at last. Verity gave a sigh of relief.

Her father attempted a laugh. 'You're imagining things.'

'No, I'm not. I thought at first that perhaps I was, but not now. I've been home for a week, long enough to be sure that there's something in the wind.' Verity studied his face, trying to find an answer there and failing.

'You've hardly seen anything of me since you've been back——'

'I know, and that's partly the point. You've always worked hard and been caught up in the business of the *estancia*, found it a challenge. But you made time to relax too. And, suddenly, you don't any more, do you? And you've a permanently preoccupied look about you, as if there's some problem that you're trying to get to grips with and not succeeding.'

Mark Williams sighed and ran a hand over his hair. It had gone a lot greyer since she was home last and Verity noticed that the lines of strain had deepened across his forehead. He was looking older, she thought with a pang. And it wasn't fair. He was only in his forties and, although he led a hard, outdoor life, it was a healthy one. It was worry that had brought this on.

'I don't know what to tell you,' he said at last.

'Why not the truth?'

He sighed again. 'It's too much to burden you with.'

'We've always faced things together, haven't we? We've been close enough for that. Don't shut me out now.'

'Yes. Since your mother died I suppose I've confided in you a lot. You've been a comfort to me, Verity.'

She felt the tears prick her eyes. Ann Williams had died of cancer four years before, but, in some ways, it seemed a very recent loss and she knew that her father still grieved deeply. She blinked hard and tried to steady herself. 'So why can't I help now?'

'I doubt if anyone could.'

It was a long time since she had heard her father so utterly despondent, and fear clutched at her. Surely it couldn't be as bad as that? 'Tell me! Please, tell me what's wrong.'

In answer he got to his feet and crossed to the old oak bureau that stood on the other side of the room. He riffled through a mess of papers and folders, found what he was looking for and returned to her. 'Read that,' he said, tossing a typewritten letter on to the table in front of her. 'It explains how matters stand better than I could.'

Verity picked it up and studied it. It wasn't a lengthy epistle, but its tone was as forceful as the nearly illegible black scrawl of a signature at the bottom of it. 'Trouble,' she agreed. 'I see what you mean. Oh, Dad, why didn't you tell me? You shouldn't have kept it to yourself.'

'I didn't want to bother you—that's why I've said nothing. I kept on hoping that something could be done, I suppose. But——'

'Is it true?'

Her father shrugged defeatedly. 'Quite true. And he's right—of course he's right. I should have faced facts long ago. It's my fault entirely.'

'That's rubbish and you know it,' she told him vehemently. 'You could do that job with one hand tied behind your back.'

'Thanks for the vote of confidence, love, but it's not well founded. Once upon a time, perhaps, when your mother was still alive. But since she died I suppose I've lost ground. Lost heart as well. Things have gone downhill and I haven't cared enough to do anything about it.'

'But he's suggesting,' Verity stabbed the letter viciously, 'that you're lazy. An incompetent idler, who's let things get in a mess.'

'They are in a mess. With the rampant inflation that

the country has been fighting for the last few years times have been hard. I haven't been able to spend money on replacing old equipment the way I once could. I've had to cut down on staff because there wasn't the money for wages. People drifted away into the towns where they were hoping for better rates of pay. And the prices we've got for stock in recent years have been way down.'

'Well, shouldn't this—this——' Verity picked up the letter again and tried to make out the signature, 'Raymond Vance, it looks like, have considered all this before putting all the blame on you?'

'It's not as simple as that. Owners of cattle ranches don't pay a manager to make excuses about the state of the economy. They expect him to take the right measures to fight back. And I haven't. It's all getting beyond my control. Sometimes I think it would take a miracle to put things back on an even footing again. I can't do it. I haven't got it in me any more.'

'So what's to be done?' Verity asked despairingly.

'It's out of my hands now. I've had warning letters before and managed to pull my socks up sufficiently for the powers-that-be in Buenos Aires to let matters ride. The owners have other business interests that occupied them and brought in money, and their man of affairs who dealt with the *estancia* was getting on in years and didn't really want to stir things up until he was forced to do something. The next thing I heard was that he'd retired and that in future a new firm would be handling matters. Obviously new brooms sweep clean. This new man wants to prove himself.'

'You'll do as he asks you?'

'I've no choice in the matter. Yes, I'll send the detailed breakdown of the ranch accounts that he's asked for. It's time the truth was out, I suppose.'

'What will happen then?' she wanted to know.

'The figures will only bear out his suspicions that there's something sadly wrong. The ranch isn't a paying proposition any more. He already guesses that I can't cope with it any longer.'

'So?'

'So I'll have to face the inevitable—the sack and the prospect of moving elsewhere for a job. Although God knows where I'll find one at my age. I'm not a young man any more and the competition is fierce.'

Verity sat in stunned silence. She thought it was bad, but nothing like as bad as this. To have to leave the only place that had ever been home to her, the gracious house that her mother had made into a warm and welcoming home, the wide-ranging pastures where she had ridden ever since she was old enough to sit astride her pony, was an appalling prospect. She just didn't want to face it. But how much more of a blow to her father, who had come here first as a newly married man in his twenties. He had worked his way up to the position of manager. It was a position of trust and he had earned it. How must he be feeling now?

She leant across and took his work-calloused hand in a comforting grasp. 'Don't worry, Dad, we'll manage somehow. It'll be all right, you'll see.' Just words, the sort of words that he had used to a small Verity when she had gone running to him with her childish problems. 'Daddy'll make it better,' he had told her then. And, somehow, he always had. But he couldn't say that any more. Now it was her turn to try to comfort him and she was at a loss.

'It's not myself I worry about as much as you.' Now that the barriers were down it was as if he couldn't stem the flood of words. 'There's your career to think about, your future. It'll be wrecked. I haven't managed to save very much over the years. If I'm out of the job I doubt there'll be enough money to pay your university fees, let alone the fare to England. I don't even know if I'll be able to give you a roof over your head any more.' There was a grey look to his face. 'Verity, can you ever forgive me for letting things get in this terrible state?'

'I blame myself for not noticing how matters were much sooner,' she said soberly. 'Perhaps I could have done something to help—left school and come back to work here. It would have been one more pair of hands around the place. If only you'd told me——' She broke off in despair. It was too late for recriminations now. It was a time to be practical and positive. 'Enough of that,' she told herself as much as her father. 'We're jumping the gun a bit, anticipating instant ruin. It doesn't have to be as black as all that. The new man may not be nearly as bad as the letter suggests. All right, he does sound a bit on his high horse, but he's not in possession of all the details yet. He's not got much to go on, so it's hardly surprising if he's rather offhand. He's—he's probably feeling his way.'

'It's a fairly assertive letter for someone who's still sizing up the situation,' Mark Williams commented sourly. 'He sounds as if he's got the picture only too clearly and just wants confirmation of his opinion before acting on it.'

'But he's never met you, never seen Vista Hermosa. He doesn't know anything about it.'

'That doesn't come into it, love. If only it did! If knowing the place and caring about it was what made the difference, things wouldn't be in the state they are.'

'It's not fair,' Verity said passionately. 'He's never ventured out of Buenos Aires in his life, I'll be bound.

What does he know about the problems you're facing? Raymond Vance—what a name!' she said scornfully. 'Can't you just see him? An old fuddy-duddy just like the previous agent they had. About sixty, going bald and with a paunch from all the business lunches he takes. He's never sat on a horse or seen a cow, and he'd run a mile if he did!'

Her father smiled at the picture she was painting. 'Maybe,' he said. 'If he *is* like the other chap, he might just leave us in peace.'

'And even if he isn't,' Verity plunged on, 'he's not got the final word, has he? What about the owners? Couldn't you talk to them and persuade them to put more money in the place? Don't they care?'

'Not a great deal, I'm afraid. In the old days when it rested with one person that might have been a possibility. But now Vista Hermosa is one of many properties owned by a big conglomerate. They delegate power to people like this Vance chap and don't really care how he runs the operation so long as it pays. If it doesn't, it's his head on the chopping block.'

'I wish it was,' said Verity with a scowl. 'Why couldn't he pick on someone else and leave us in peace instead of poking his nose in where he isn't wanted?'

'Why indeed?' her father echoed. 'But that doesn't help. The fact is that he has chosen to interfere and he has the authority to do so. I'll send the information he wants tomorrow, and then we'll wait for further developments.' For her sake he pinned on a smile. 'You may be right—it may all be a storm in a teacup.'

'Of course I'm right!' Verity injected as much confidence as she could into her voice. 'We'll look back on this episode in a couple of years' time and wonder why we worried.'

But later, as she undressed and got ready for bed in

the small room overlooking the stables that had been hers since childhood, she felt considerably less certain about the future. It was all very well to sound optimistic about the future in an effort to cheer her father, but what if the worst happened and this overlord, hundreds of miles away, exercised his power on the owners' behalf and decided that it was best to replace her father with a younger man, someone with modern ideas and lots of drive and energy?

Verity knew enough about the world of big business to realise that people did not matter when it was a question of finance and hard business tactics. In that world, so remote from their own little backwater, anyone who didn't pull his weight was weeded out mercilessly. She shivered. Her imagination took over. Would they end up walking the streets? Plenty of people did, she knew, even in a supposedly wealthy country like Argentina. They came up to you as you went shopping, their hands outstretched as they pleaded for 'just a few pesos, señorita, to buy food'. They were the old, the crippled and society's other rejects, those who could not find work or who did not want to. How often had she felt in her purse for a coin or two to give them. Perhaps she might be one of the ones on the receiving end in a very short while.

She gave herself a mental shake. That was foolish. She was getting carried away by self-pity, Verity told herself. She was young and she was strong and, in the unlikely event of her father looking for another job and failing to find one, she would get some kind of work herself. It would only be a temporary measure. She could be a maid or a cleaner; they were always in demand, it seemed. Or work in a shop. It was a pity that, in spite of the best education that was available in her part of the world, she wasn't actually better qualified for life, she thought ruefully.

At the convent she had attended the nuns had said that she was a joy to teach and had prophesied an academic career of some kind for her. She might go into teaching herself, for she had always loved children. Or perhaps publishing or journalism. And her father, when she had put it to him, had encouraged her all the way. There was none of the male chauvinist about him. Although her mother had been satisfied with her quiet domestic life on the *estancia*, caring for her husband and child, if Verity wanted a career and a chance to see the world beyond there was no way Mark Williams would stand in her path.

'That's not to say that I don't hope you'll meet the right man one day and settle down with him to make me a grandfather if the mood takes you,' he had joked, and she had teased him about it.

'You're not old enough by a long chalk to think about being a grandfather yet,' she had laughed. 'Wait until you've got white hair and a stoop and really look the part!'

She supposed he did now. That was what worry did to you. The bright chestnut hair—something that she had inherited from him—had dulled to a uniform grey that held nothing of her own glorious colouring. 'No doubt whose daughter you are,' her mother had laughed more than once. 'The same hair, the same dark eyes with tawny glints, the same spare frame, not an ounce of flesh going begging on either of you.'

She hadn't changed very much in that respect, thought Verity, smiling faintly. Her face had lost its childish scrawniness and had developed instead a fine, high-cheekboned look that might have passed for beauty if it hadn't been accompanied by a nose that no one could call anything but snub and a mouth that was much too wide. And as for the rest of her! Argentinian men liked their girls nicely rounded in the places where it counted. No one in his right mind would look at her. No, she would stay single and dwindle into an old maid. As she finally drifted off to sleep in the early hours of the morning Verity dreamt that she was being wooed by an ageing Lothario in a tail coat who was telling her in a quavering voice, 'Marry me, why don't you? It's your last chance, you know. Your last chance of happiness.' As she pushed him away from her with a gesture of revulsion, she noticed that he had a name tag on his lapel. It was Raymond Vance.

For the rest of the week Verity and her father kept their talk to safely neutral subjects, determinedly avoiding the matter that was uppermost in both their minds. Mark Williams spent two long evenings bringing his ranch accounts up to date, assembling the information that Raymond Vance had requested. Verity helped him as far as she could, secretly horrified by the mess that was revealed. The package was sent off, she volunteered to take it to the post office in Campo Verde, the nearest town, herself.

Then the waiting began. A day to reach Buenos Aires, maybe two or three if there was some hold-up in the mail as was often the case, even with air deliveries. Then he would have to have time to study everything before he decided what action, if any, to take. It had to be at least a week, say ten days to be on the safe side, before they could even expect to hear from the man, perhaps longer if he was as long-winded as most of his kind and had other work on hand. It would not matter to him that the result of his deliberations was awaited with desperate eagerness at Vista Hermosa. Something in the lazy scrawl of his signature suggested a fair indifference to the views of others, Verity decided.

Mark Williams adopted a fatalistic attitude. Now that his worries were out in the open and he was no longer hiding anything from his daughter he seemed almost happy, and she could tell that a good half of the burden had been concealing it from her. Now he threw himself into the business of the *estancia* with more enthusiasm than Verity had seen in him for a long time, setting off to organise the cattle-dipping programme that took place every January as part of the regular campaign against disease.

Her father wasn't really happy as an administrator, thought Verity as she watched him go, riding off with the team of *gauchos*, the hardened men of the *pampas*, who spoke little but rode like the wind and understood cattle and their ways probably better than they did their fellow human beings. They would be gone all day, rounding up animals in the far pastures, driving them in to pen them near the dipping troughs and then back again to the rich grazing grounds miles from the main ranch. It was taxing work, requiring hard physical effort, but it brought its own rewards. 'There's nothing like a life spent close to the land,' her father had told her once and, seeing the satisfaction he got after a day in the saddle, she could believe him.

Not that it was women's work. Verity accepted that. *Machismo*, that indefinable word that suggested a combination of brute strength and sexual vigour, in South American terms the ultimate qualities a man should possess, forbade any interference by the so-called weaker sex. To be out on the plains pitting his wits and testing his strength against the animal world and the elements was a man's destiny. Verity knew how appalled her father's workers would have been if she had ever tried to invade their territory. To a *gaucho* a woman had other uses.

It was a lovely day, sunny, but not too hot, with a breeze that drifted pleasantly through the avenue of eucalyptus trees that led to the house. Verity watched the men ride out until they were dust specks in the distance, then sighed and turned back towards the house. She would have given anything to have saddled up the horse that was kept for her own use and to have taken off for the day herself. She had often done that in the past, spending happy hours on her own. On a ranch the size of Vista Hermosa one could ride all day without seeing another soul, without even reaching the boundary fences.

But there was work to be done indoors and, with a shrug, she made her way to the kitchen and collected her cleaning materials. When she was at home, on holiday from the school where she had been a boarder, Verity had always made the housework her responsibility. Her father made an effort to keep the rooms that he used clean and relatively tidy, but there was usually a great deal to be done.

This time was no exception. Her father had lived mainly in the old-fashioned, spacious kitchen, using it for eating, the minimal amount of office work that he did and for relaxing and listening to the radio in his rare free time. Apart from his bedroom which was reasonably clean the rest of the house had been allowed to go to rack and ruin. Verity had determined that in this year that she would be spending at home with him before she went to university she would make a real effort to turn the place into the home that it had been when her mother had been alive.

And just because some interfering old man in Buenos Aires might evict them, it was no reason at all to change her plans, she told herself firmly. She headed for the

sala, a handsome room at the front of the house where
they had sometimes entertained in the days when her
mother had enjoyed meeting their neighbours from
adjoining *estancias* and sometimes folk from farther
afield.

It was a long time since anything of that sort had
taken place, Verity thought, as she wielded her cleaning
cloth vigorously. Clouds of accumulated dust rose and
she coughed and sneezed as she worked. She had
wrapped a scarf round her hair and she had her oldest
dress on, a shabby affair that should have been discarded years ago. But it was comfortable and shapeless
and she had hung on to it. She must look nearly as
much of a disaster area as the room itself, she decided,
as she pressed on. Thank goodness they didn't have
callers these days!

It was then that she heard the car. She went to the
window and peered out. It was probably a false alarm.
They weren't expecting anyone. Except—unless it
was—— No, that was impossible. There would be all
sorts of things to arrange before Raymond Vance sent
someone to the ranch to organise matters.

But the car *was* coming to Vista Hermosa. She saw
the Land Rover turn off the smooth-surfaced road, a
cloud of dust accompanying it as it bumped its way up
the unmade track that led past the stockyards and
dipping pens and wound finally up through the sadly
overgrown gardens, once her mother's pride and joy,
to the *estancia*. There the driver pulled to a halt, the
engine stopped and a stranger got out and strode
quickly towards the flight of shallow steps that led to
the house.

Verity did not know much about men, but she knew
that this one meant trouble the moment that she set
eyes on him. Trouble of a kind that her short and

hitherto sheltered life had not prepared her to recognise until now—let alone deal with. But the experiences of the last few days had taught her a thing or two about the knocks that life could throw at one out of a clear sky.

He was tall, very tall by Argentinian standards, six foot at least, Verity judged with a powerful, broad-shouldered frame honed to a hard-muscled perfection that, with his deeply tanned face, suggested someone who was used to an active, outdoor life, although the immaculately white linen he wore, the well-cut dark suit that moulded itself to his form, the polished perfection of his shoes and the heavy gold watch that he sported on one wrist all made it transparently clear that this was no mere *peon*, but a man of standing. He was in his early thirties, she supposed, and something about the arrogant set of his dark head and the unsmiling line of his mouth told her more clearly than words could have done that this was a man who would brook no opposition to his authority.

Verity heard his step outside, an amazingly light tread for so big a man, and then the sound of a decisive rap on the front door. She had a sudden- feeling of blind panic and hesitated on her way to answer it, strangely reluctant to confront him, whoever he was. Perhaps he would go away, if she did nothing, remained silent within doors. Something inside her was warning her that this stranger was bringing upheaval to her tidy life and she didn't like the prospect.

She should have known that he wasn't the sort of man to be denied like that. He waited for a moment or two, then knocked again, and, after a brief pause, again, as if he was getting impatient. Then the handle turned and he walked in. Verity hadn't expected that. A shaft of sunlight from the open door pinned her where she stood amid the dim shadows of the entrance hall, poised for flight, but too startled to run any- where.

'So there was someone here. You certainly took your time about answering the door.' He spoke in Spanish, his voice cool, accustomed to command. 'I want to speak with Señor Williams. Is he here or out with the men?'

He had taken her for a servant. Hardly surprising, Verity thought, as she stood there in her out-of-date dress, clutching the duster she had been using to her breast as if in self-defence.

The cold, brusque voice sounded again. 'Well? You've a tongue in your head, I imagine? Señor Williams, where is he?'

She answered automatically in the same language; she had spoken Spanish as easily as English from the age of three and all her schooling had been in that tongue. 'He's not here. He's——' She found this man too overwhelming for comfort at such close quarters. Somehow the right words deserted her, stuck in her throat.

The stranger broke in impatiently, 'I suppose not, at this time of day. Any reasonable man would have been at work long since—it's to be hoped so, at any rate. Do you expect him back for lunch or is he gone for the day? Where is he? Near the house? Rounding up stock? Is there someone else you could send to fetch him or are you on your own here?'

The questions came as thick and as fast as burst of gunfire and Verity struggled to reply. 'Yes—no—that is, there's no one here but me. You see——'

He shrugged. 'And you, heaven help us, wouldn't win any prizes in an intelligence contest,' he said to himself in an undertone. She flinched at the description and he noticed the action. She had an idea that this man didn't miss very much. 'Oh, you understood that, did you?' He didn't apologise for the remark and she hardly expected him to. After all, she had been behaving like some kind of halfwit. But he had taken her so much off balance that it was an effort to think straight.

'What's your business with Señor Williams?' she asked. The words came out more belligerently than she had intended, and a dark brow rose quizzically in reaction.

'I don't think that's any of your concern. It's between him and me. Now, for the last time of asking, where is he?'

'Find out for yourself!' Her temper flared suddenly. Just who exactly was this arrogant stranger and what right had he to be bawling her out like this? She wasn't going to put up with such rudeness. Verity turned on her heel. She didn't know where she was going, only that she had to get away from him before she did something really disastrous, like slapping his goodlooking face.

He took two strides after her and seized her arm in a rough grasp, spinning her round to face him. 'I intend to find out,' he said grimly, 'whatever means I have to use on you to get the information.'

She felt a cold trickle of fear go down her spine. What was he going to do to her? What on earth had possessed her to tell him that she was alone in the house?

'Well?' His eyes were dark and as cold as ice chips and she stared at them as if mesmerised. He shook her impatiently. 'I'm waiting for an answer, damn you,' he said. 'It's important. It matters a good deal to me.'

'Does it? And just who exactly are you that you expect everyone to dance to your piping?' she asked angrily.

His grip tightened on her almost unbearably and she could feel anger in him, tightly checked. 'The name is Vance,' he said.

CHAPTER TWO

'VANCE?' Verity was stunned and her face showed it. '*You're* Raymond Vance?' Was this vital and aggressive hunk of manhood the elderly businessman that she had imagined and described so clearly to her father? It just did not seem possible.

'Ramón Vance,' he corrected.

Ramón, not Raymond. Yes, that made sense. On paper it was easy to confuse the two. But, in the flesh, there was nothing remotely English about the man who stood before her except the excellence with which he spoke the language. He was a tough, hard Spanish-American with a no-nonsense approach to life.

'You seem surprised,' he said stiffly. He released her numbed arm and she stepped back from him, rubbing it to restore the circulation.

'I am. You're not what we pictured at all after reading your letter.'

'I see. Has speculation been rife?' he asked grimly. 'I didn't realise that Mark Williams made a habit of sharing his personal mail with the servants.'

That was a misapprehension that she had not had a chance to correct yet. She supposed she had better introduce herself. 'No, Mr Vance, he doesn't. But——'

'But your position is a more privileged one, is it?' The dark glance raked over her contemptuously. 'I understand that Mrs Williams died some time ago——' He paused significantly.

What was he suggesting? He surely didn't think that she was—that her father would—— Hysteria fought with blind rage at the insinuation. 'How dare you? I'm Mark Williams' daughter!' She moved towards him, her hand raised to slap the superior expression off the dark face in front of her. 'You swine—you——'

He anticipated the action. 'I shouldn't, if you know what's good for you,' he warned, catching her easily and fending her off with the minimum of effort before she could carry out her intention.

'I've never been so insulted in my life!' she spat at him.

'You haven't lived very long. If that's the worst anyone ever throws at you, you're lucky,' he said smoothly. 'It was an understandable mistake in the circumstances.'

'Really? I didn't think gentlemen made mistakes like that.'

He laughed harshly. 'Don't fool yourself. I'm no gentleman.'

'Apparently not,' she snapped, 'if that's all you're prepared to offer by way of an apology.'

'I'm not in the habit of apologising for my actions.' He dismissed the matter. 'And you still have the advantage of me in the way of names.'

Verity seethed. But there was nothing that she could do. She stood about as much chance of besting him physically as a fly beating itself against a steel wall, probably less. 'I'm Verity Williams,' she told him sulkily.

He gave her a curt nod of acknowledgment. 'Now that the formal introductions have been effected, do we have to stand here in the entrance hall for ever?'

He had a knack of putting her in the wrong. She felt like a six-year-old, reprimanded for bad manners. 'Of course not. Perhaps you'd care to come into the *sala*?'

A morning's cleaning had made less of an impact on

the room than Verity had hoped and, after one appalled look, he asked in disgust, 'Is there nowhere else?'

She shrugged. 'We use the back room, mainly.'

'It can't be worse than this,' he said distastefully. 'We'll go there.'

'All right.' She wasn't going to argue with him about it. At least the room was clean and reasonably tidy. She had done it out yesterday, ignoring her father's protests that he would never be able to find anything again. She led the way.

She couldn't tell from his expression whether this room pleased him any better. He gave it another of the sharp, searching looks that she was becoming to associate with him and then turned back to her. 'I could use a cup of coffee and something to eat.' It was an order, not a request, and she bridled instinctively. 'I've had nothing since a snatched breakfast early this morning.'

She felt like saying, 'Too bad. Don't expect me to feed you.' But she had the feeling that he was quite capable of putting her over his knee and spanking her like a small, disobedient child, if she tried anything of the sort. 'I'll see what I can find,' she said in a grudging tone, and headed for the kitchen, aware of his gaze following her as she went through the alcove into the adjoining room.

It didn't take her long to brew a pot of coffee and cut a pile of sandwiches. If he was expecting anything in the Cordon Bleu line, it was just too bad, she thought furiously. She put the food on a tray and carried the lot back into the room, banging it unceremoniously down on the dining table.

Ramón Vance stood with his back to her looking through the window past the sheds that clustered round the back of the house to the plains beyond. Vista

Hermosa: beautiful prospect. The original owner had named the place for that view across the lush grasses of the *pampas*, and even today's neglect could not detract from the description. It was still enough to make Verity catch her breath when she met it unexpectedly, even after all the years that she had lived here. She wondered what Ramón Vance made of it all. Had he ever seen anything like it?

He turned and, without waiting for an invitation, seated himself in her father's favourite chair, a button-backed leather piece that had seen better days, but which was at least comfortable. 'You can put the tray over here,' he commanded, indicating the small table by the side of the chair.

He spoke as if she was indeed the servant he had mistaken her for at first sight. Verity bit back the tart reply that sprang to her lips and could tell from the sudden glint in his eyes that he knew exactly how she was feeling. Damn the man for his perception! She picked up the tray and deposited it where he had requested with another ungracious bang and rattle of crockery.

'Thank you,' he said. 'I've often heard about the overwhelming hospitality of the folk who live on the *pampas*. It's nice to see it in action.'

She shifted uneasily at the mockery in his tone. How soon could she make her escape from him and give herself time to recover her composure? She glanced longingly at the door. Would he want to be left alone while he ate his meal?

'Have you eaten yet?' His voice interrupted her thoughts.

The prospect of sharing a meal with the man revolted her. 'I'm not hungry,' she told him shortly— and as if to give the lie to her statement her stomach rumbled loudly in protest.

He shrugged. 'Please yourself. Then you can sit and watch me.'

'I'd rather——' she began hastily.

His eyes met her dark ones. 'I'm not concerned with what you'd rather do,' he said softly. 'Sit down.'

'You've no right to order me about!'

'I've every right. Now, are you going to sit down or do I have to come over to you and see that you do as I tell you. And, believe me, I will.'

He meant business. She could tell that from his tone, although he hadn't raised his voice. He didn't need to. She complied, perching nervously on the edge of one of the hard, upright dining chairs, her hands folded primly in front of her like a little girl. After all, if that was the way that he was determined to treat her, what was the point of trying to act any differently?

He poured himself a cup of coffee and its fragrance wafted tantalisingly over to her. 'Want a cup?' he asked.

'No, thank you,' she said.

He ate one sandwich and bit hungrily into another. 'These are good,' he told her.

'We aim to please.' She wasn't accepting any olive branches, if that was what he intended. Did he think he could sweet-talk her round with remarks like that? Her mouth curved scornfully at the thought.

'I'm glad to hear it. I must admit that I haven't noticed much evidence of your desire to please so far. Tell me,' he said pleasantly, 'are you always this bloody-minded with visitors, or have you something special against me?'

'What do you think?' she asked him provocatively. She was a fool to bait him, she knew, but something drove her to it.

'I think you're going to land yourself in a load of trouble, if you're not careful.'

'Stop talking to me as if I was a child!' she flared angrily.

'Then stop acting like one.' He got to his feet and she tensed. What was he going to do? Surely he wouldn't dare lay a finger on her? Her face must have mirrored her thoughts accurately, because he laughed unpleasantly. 'You're not so bold as you make out, are you? All fire and fury, but no guts when it comes down to it.' He divided the sandwiches on his plate and brought a half share over to her. 'You'll eat these,' he commanded.

'I've already told you——' she began rebelliously.

'You'll eat them whether you're hungry or not. And get yourself a cup and have some coffee too. You've wasted enough of my time already.'

Verity found herself obeying him meekly. She hadn't really backed down, she told herself, as she bit ravenously into the food, relishing every mouthful. It was just that there was no point making a heavy issue out of something so relatively unimportant. She met his faintly mocking gaze as she drained her cup of coffee and wondered who she was fooling. It certainly wasn't him.

'Now,' her persecutor said, when she had finished, 'we have to talk.'

'What do you want to talk about?' she asked defensively. 'I've nothing to tell you.'

'I think you could tell me a great deal if it suited you.'

'Perhaps it doesn't suit me, then,' she countered.

'No, it probably doesn't. You're an awkward brat—that's one fact I've established without any digging,' he said nastily. 'What are you doing here anyway? I thought you were away at school.'

'You're very well informed!'

'I make it my business to be.'

She supposed there was no harm in explaining how things stood. It wasn't of vital importance anyway. 'I left school at the end of the term before last,' she admitted.

'And it's now January. What did you do in between?'

'A finishing course. It was run by an academy in Cordoba. We learnt deportment, etiquette, housecraft, how to entertain——'

'Spare me the details. I think I know the sort of thing,' he said rudely. 'You don't seem to have profited too much from it.'

'You, of all people, can hardly expect the red carpet treatment,' she told him resentfully. 'You're hardly a welcome visitor.'

'Somehow I didn't think I would be. Tell me, did the previous agent get the same sort of reception?'

'He never came to Vista Hermosa. He stayed in Buenos Aires and didn't poke his nose in where he wasn't wanted.'

'Very right and proper by your standards,' he mocked her. 'And, meanwhile, the *estancia* continued on its merry path to rack and ruin. But that wouldn't worry you, of course.'

'I wouldn't know about that,' she said defensively.

'No, of course not. You were away at school, weren't you? How convenient for you! Well, I would know. I've done my homework on the subject. And I'm far from satisfied with what's going on here. I suppose your father must have filled you in on how matters stood when he showed you my letter?'

Verity gave what she hoped was a careless shrug of

her shoulders. There was no sense in letting him know into what confusion that letter had cast them. 'He said there were a few problems. Nothing that can't be ironed out fairly quickly, I imagine.'

'Do you? And when did you study cattle-farming?'

'I don't need to,' she said haughtily.

'No? You go on instinct, I suppose,' he asked sarcastically.

'I trust my father's judgment,' she snapped back at him.

'I'm glad someone's got some faith in him.'

'Meaning you haven't?'

Irritatingly, he checked himself and retrieved the temper that he had seemed in imminent danger of losing. It would have been satisfying if she had made him drop that air of cool superiority, Verity thought. 'Don't put words in my mouth,' he warned her.

'It's true, isn't it,' she said bitterly. 'It was there in every line of that letter you wrote. You don't believe in him, do you?'

'I don't know your father, so I can't judge.'

'No, you don't know him. Well, let me tell you, Mr Vance, he's worth ten of you! He's decent and hard-working and honest and——'

'He may be all of those things,' Ramón Vance agreed smoothly. 'And, if he is, there may be some other reason for the *estancia* profits going downhill in the last few years. Whatever it is, I'm here to find out the cause. With your permission, of course.'

What a sarcastic beast he was, thought Verity. She had never met anyone that she disliked quite as much as she disliked this man. 'You belittle my farming knowledge and I've lived here all my life—long enough to have picked up a fair amount of practical information about cattle and the way they behave. What does a city slicker like yourself know? Have you even seen ranch cattle outside pictures in books or on the screen?' she asked him scornfully.

'I know enough to get by,' he said, but didn't seem inclined to expand on the remark.

'We weren't expecting a visit from you,' she added.

'So I'd gathered. I can't think why, it was the obvious course to take. But there's no need to apologise about that.' His tone was very bland and she raised her chin defiantly in reaction.

'I'm not apologising, I was just——'

'Yes?'

'Explaining why I was surprised to see you,' she said lamely. 'I expect my father would have stayed at home if he'd known you were arriving. But I suppose that was deliberate on your part.'

He didn't pretend to misunderstand her. 'Arriving out of the blue, you mean. Perhaps. Another example of my underhand nature which you find so different from your father.'

'As you say.' She tossed her head, her chestnut hair escaping untidily from the confines of the scarf that she wound round it and had determinedly not removed in the visitor's presence. 'You'll see that I'm right when you meet him.'

'And when *do* I get to meet this paragon?' he asked. 'Rewarding as I find it bandying words with you, it's not my primary objective at the moment. As far as I remember, I asked you where your father was within the first few seconds of our meeting. It's now,' he consulted his watch, 'nearly forty-five minutes later and we still haven't established his whereabouts.'

Verity capitulated. There was no point stalling for time. The sooner the two men met, the sooner this arrogant stranger could revise his opinion of her father.

'Dad's out on a round-up over near the Los Molinos boundary,' she said. 'They left early, but I don't expect them back for a while yet.' She studied the visitor doubtfully. 'It's a good way and I don't know which route they'll take back. Can you ride? I could come with you and show you the way, but we might miss them, even so. This isn't Palermo Park in Buenos Aires, you know, tame and civilised. It's vast. You get lost quite easily if you're not familiar with the land-marks. I've done it myself, and I've been riding round here since I was a little girl.'

'And I'm sure you'd weep bitter tears if I did,' he mocked her. 'So when do you expect them back?'

'Two hours, maybe three. It depends if there've been any problems. He'll want to have the cattle secured in the pens before nightfall so that dipping can start first thing tomorrow. We do it in batches, you know.'

Ramón Vance nodded. Verity couldn't tell whether all this was new to him or not. 'There's no point riding out. He'll be fully occupied with the job in hand and won't thank me for interfering at a time like that.'

Verity doubted if her father would want him inter-fering at any time, but refrained from saying as much. 'You'll take a rest,' she suggested hopefully. 'I expect you're tired after your journey.' She could certainly do with a break from him.

She wondered if he numbered mind-reading among his talents as his eyes met hers briefly and lit with the inner mockery that never seemed far below the surface with him. 'I'm sorry to disappoint you, but no, I don't want a rest. It takes more than a one-hour flight in a well-equipped plane, followed by a shortish drive and reasonable roads, to throw me off balance. Although,' he slanted a wicked look at her, 'I'll admit that the last hour has been a little on the hectic side.'

She wouldn't rise to that one. Instead she said stiffly, 'What would you like to do, Mr Vance?' Perhaps if she froze him off with icy politeness she might find him easier to deal with.

'You're giving me a free rein?'

'It looks as if I haven't got much option,' she shrugged.

'Not a lot,' he agreed. 'So show me the house. I want to see every part of it from the roof to the cellars, if there are any. I don't want anything missed out. Is that understood?'

'Crystal clear,' she said through gritted teeth.

Two hours later Verity could well believe his claim that he didn't tire easily. They had toured the house from top to bottom and from end to end. He had even inspected the gardens. And, as they went along, the sight of each new room inspired more questions, most of which she found herself totally incapable of answering. This man covered points that she had never even thought about before. How long since the roof was last overhauled? Were the unused bedrooms aired regularly? The mattresses in those rooms, were they originals, dating from the first owner's time, or had they been replaced since? Which herbs were in the overgrown garden? Were they ever used? And what about entertainment? Did they do a lot? Had they done in the past?

They returned to the living room at the back of the house where the tour had begun, and Verity could not conceal her weariness as she slumped into an easy chair.

'Tired?' he asked, with a noticeable lack of sympathy in his voice. 'Have I been too hard on you?'

As if he would care if he had! She suspected that Ramón Vance had enjoyed watching her flounder

under his barrage of questions. She had not come out of the inquisition too well, and they were both aware of the fact.

She wondered what was next on the agenda. Normally she would have been thinking about preparations for dinner. She enjoyed cooking and, after his usual diet of beef, beef, and more beef, done in a fairly unimaginative way, when he was on his own Mark Williams was an always appreciative sampler of her efforts.

The visitor's thoughts seemed to be moving in the same direction, however. 'You look as if it would take a major earthquake to get you out of that chair,' he began in a deceptively soft tone.

That, or a couple of sarcastic words from him, Verity thought. 'But?' she said.

'But there's an evening meal to get ready.'

'So there is,' she agreed. If she was wise, she knew that she ought to hang on to the shreds of her temper and disappear into the kitchen, docility personified. But Verity had never been one to take the easy way out. It didn't come with her colour hair. 'But I'm tired.'

'Doesn't that wonderful father of yours merit a decent meal when he gets home after a hard day in the saddle?'

'He'll understand.'

'Will he? Well, he may put up with your moods, but I won't.'

'If you're so keen on eating why don't you do something about it?' she challenged him.

'I fully intend to.' Before she knew exactly what was happening to her he was across the room, jerking her roughly to her feet and forcing her towards the kitchen.

'Let me go, you swine!' She struggled impotently against the steel strength of his arms, kicking out wildly at his legs in an attempt to get him to release her. She might just as well have saved her energy; her efforts got her precisely nowhere.

'Is that the sort of behaviour you learn't at finishing school?' he taunted her as, with one twist of his wrist, he ensured her surrender.

'Damn you!' she shouted furiously, forced to lean back against his hard, unyielding body, the fight knocked out of her. *He* was not even breathing any faster; the tussle had left him unmoved.

'Well, are you going to prepare the meal or not?' The hateful voice reached her again. 'I've been fairly kind to you so far, but, if you want to play rough——'

'No,' she said. She knew when she was beaten and he had got the better of her this time.

'You'll do the cooking?'

'I'll do the cooking,' she agreed, and found herself free.

'What time do you and your father usually eat?'

'About seven,' Verity said. 'I know you've barely finished afternoon tea at that time in Buenos Aires, but we don't keep city hours here. We're up at first light and in bed early at night. There's work to be done.'

He ignored the gibe. 'All right, seven o'clock it is. Can you cook?'

'You'll have to wait and see, won't you? I don't suppose I'll come up to your high standards, will I? I suppose all the women that you know are Cordon Bleu cooks?'

'Some of them,' he said with faint amusement. 'But, generally speaking, I don't pick my escorts for their ability in the kitchen.'

No, for their expertise in quite another department, Verity decided. If he was trying to embarrass her, he wouldn't succeed. She might not have much practical experience of meeting men and dealing with them, but she had read enough to know just what he meant. Well, he would get a rough reception if he tried any of *that* sort of thing on her!

He was two feet away from her now, leaning casually against the door-jamb, but, somehow, he was still too close for comfort. His nearness overpowered her, overwhelmed her in a way that she had not known before, and she wanted to distance herself from him to dispel the effect. She moved back into the room and winced as she did so. Did he have to be so—so physical?

'Did I hurt you?' he asked.

'What do you think? I'll have bruises all over me by tomorrow,' she told him resentfully.

'That's your own fault entirely. Perhaps they'll serve as a reminder to you in the future not to fight the inevitable.'

'I should give in gracefully, you mean. Yes, Mr Vance. No, Mr Vance. Three bags full, Mr Vance,' she snapped. 'Is that what you want?'

'It would come as a pleasant surprise in your case,' he admitted.

'You may get that sort of treatment from your other women, but you won't hear it from me!'

'We'll see,' he said lazily.

'Will we?' she challenged him. '*I* don't think so.'

He shrugged. He wasn't going to make an issue of it, thank goodness. He was studying her, as if comparing her with his usual female escorts and finding her wanting, and Verity felt an irrational pang of wounded female pride. So she didn't look glamorous just at the moment. No one would after being manhandled like that! She wasn't a pampered city girl, forever at the beauty salon and alarmed if the wind blew her hair out of place. But, when she was trying, she didn't look bad. She had her moments, even if she couldn't give his women a run for their money. Not that she would want to, she thought scornfully. They were welcome to him!

'I'll leave you to produce the meal of the century.' Ramón Vance straightened and turned away.

'What are you going to do?' Was he intending to turn his attention to some other area where the Williams family would be found to be slack and lazy?

'Did you want me to keep you company in the kitchen?' His voice mocked her. 'Somehow, I thought you would have had enough of me for the moment.'

'Oh, I have. More than enough. But I——'

'But you don't want me snooping around on my own discovering any more of your father's sins of omission. Is that it?'

He read her like a book, she thought furiously, wondering how to retrieve the situation. He was too clever by half. Why did it have to be him? Why couldn't it have been an elderly businessman with an eye to a pretty girl whom she could have twisted round her finger with ease? She very much doubted if any woman could get the better of Ramón Vance.

'I'm going for a stroll outside,' he informed her. 'Do you think that will keep me out of harm's way?'

'If you keep out of *my* way, I don't care where you get to,' she flared at him, no longer caring about his intentions. If he wanted to pry, he would. There was nothing much she could do to stop him.

He laughed, a deep and unexpectedly attractive sound. 'I'll try not to be late for dinner,' he said. 'Oh, and Verity——'

It was the first time that he had used her christian name, and she stiffened. 'Yes?' she snapped. 'What is it now?'

'You might tidy yourself up a little. It would pay you.'

'Would it really?'

'Yes. I can always forgive culinary disasters if the woman who perpetrated them makes an effort in other directions. You're a mess at the moment, but I imagine you could be quite presentable if you put your mind to it.'

And, giving her no opportunity to respond to that calculated piece of provocation, he vanished in the direction of the gardens, leaving Verity no solace except that of banging saucepans about as she wished that she could throw them at Ramón Vance's arrogant head.

CHAPTER THREE

TIME did not cool Verity's feelings. If anything it fanned the flames. She woke early next morning and lay, still half asleep, enjoying the sunlight streaming into her room and giving promise of another perfect January day. Then she groaned aloud as the realisation struck her. There was a large cloud on the horizon, in the shape of Ramón Vance.

She did not think that she had ever disliked anyone quite as much as him. And, last night, she had made no secret of the fact. Not that he had cared. He had treated her like the spoiled brat that he obviously considered her. She did not mind about that; but what did matter was that her father had seemed to agree with him. She frowned at the thought. How dared the man make trouble between her and her father?

She had got the meal under way, taking her time over the preparations in the hope that her father would arrive and give her the opportunity for a quick warning talk about their visitor before formal introductions were made. But eventually, realising that he had clearly been delayed, she was forced to abandon the idea and retreat to her room in one of the side wings of the house to make herself presentable for dinner.

She took a quick bath in the antiquated bathroom that was one of four in the house, but the only one in reasonable working order, then surveyed her wardrobe for something suitable to wear. She pulled a face as she looked at the selection on offer. Usually she lived in jeans and T-shirts outdoors, ringing the changes in the evening with a few cotton dresses, most of which she had run up herself on her mother's ancient sewing-machine. There was not a thing that would come up to Ramón Vance's exacting standards.

Her hand strayed towards her plainly-cut gingham school dress. Why not? After all, he had treated her like a child all day. She slipped it on, and, with an impish grin, set about braiding her hair. She looked about twelve, she thought, surveying the result with pleasure. Well, it would serve him right! He was used to women who made an effort to please him and dressed accordingly. Here was one at least who had no intention of doing any such thing and she didn't care a hoot about signalling the fact to him loud and clear.

She looked at her watch. Six-thirty, and *he* had said that they would dine at seven. On the dot, if she knew anything about the man. Verity hoped that her father was not going to be held up. The prospect of dining alone with Ramón Vance was not a pleasant one. As she made her way back to the main part of the house she heard the sound of Mark Williams' voice and gave a quick sigh of relief. That was one danger averted.

'Dad!' she called. 'You're back at last, thank goodness! The most awful thing has happened——' She broke off in horror as she realised that he was talking, not, as she had supposed, to one of his men, but to Ramón Vance.

Both men turned at the interruption and she skidded to a halt in front of them, the rest of her unwise speech hastily swallowed.

'Verity!' Her father's look of surprised disapproval showed what he thought of her outburst. He cast a faintly apologetic look at the man by his side. 'I'm sorry, Mr Vance. My daughter tends to speak without thinking——'

'I'd noticed already. A trait that the very young have, wouldn't you agree? Discretion comes with maturity.' Ramón Vance's dark eyes slid over her changed appearance with faint distaste.

'You should have shown Mr Vance to the guest room, Verity,' Mark Williams reproached her. 'He'll want to freshen up before dinner, I expect. I know I certainly need to.' He looked down at his working clothes, dusty and smelling of horses, contrasting strongly with the immaculate appearance of the visitor. 'I'll leave you in Verity's capable hands, if you'll excuse me.' The brief glance he gave his daughter indicated that there would be trouble ahead if her treatment of their guest was less than gracious. 'She can be the perfect hostess when she tries.'

'Except that you're not trying at the moment, are you?' Ramón Vance said softly as they were left alone. 'I suppose *that*,' he waved a contemptuous hand towards her dress, 'is supposed to provoke me, is it?'

'And does it?' she asked him sweetly.

'Not in the way you imagine,' he told her, his gaze roving over her figure, making her suddenly aware that last year's school clothes sat a little tightly on this year's more mature figure. The swell of her firm young breasts strained slightly at the buttons of the dress and the hem revealed a little more of her shapely legs than was fashionable, or, as she suddenly realised, indeed decent.

'Don't look at me like that,' she said, absurdly self-conscious.

'If you will walk round looking like an overgrown Shirley Temple, you must expect people to stare at you.' He gave a mocking laugh. 'I don't suppose I'm the only man to react that way.'

'You're horrid,' she said childishly.

'So I've been told, times without number.' He did not sound as if it bothered him. 'Now, what about doing as your father said like the dutiful child that you are and showing me to my room?'

Verity stalked off in the direction from which she had just come. 'It's this way,' she said as rudely as she dared, continuing on her way toward the guest room and not deigning to look behind her to see if he was following or not.

Verity had not realised how shabby the guest room was these days. It was so rarely used that no one had thought to bother slapping a coat of paint on the walls or replacing the faded curtains. The occasional representative from a company supplying cattle feed or chemical products stayed the night and school friends of her own had spent weekends there, but the rest of the time it was largely forgotten. She even skimped on its cleaning.

Ramón Vance walked past her into the room. 'How charming! And so in keeping with the character of the rest of the house,' he commented dryly as he looked at the dust that lay thickly on top of a chest of drawers.

'I don't have time to attend to everything,' she said defensively. 'It's a big house. When my father first lived here twenty years ago the *estancia* had a staff of forty. There were four men just to look after the gardens. Can you imagine it? And there was a housekeeper and maids to run the house. It was properly run then.'

'Times change.' He tested the bed with one hand and the springs groaned protestingly.

'And not for the better,' she told him. 'In the old days the owner cared what happened at the ranch even if he didn't actually live here. Now it's all handed over on a plate to someone like you.'

'Are you saying that I don't care? I thought that was

why I was here—to find out why the place isn't paying its way any longer.'

'Money! Profits! That's all that people like you think about, isn't it? There are more important things in life,' she flared at him.

'Not many,' he said calmly. 'What paid for your fancy schooling? What is it that clothes you, feeds you, gives you a chance in life? I think you'd be a little lost without it, for all your fine words.'

'You wouldn't understand, of course,' Verity told him. 'It's no use talking to you.'

'Perhaps not,' he agreed. 'I'm an insensitive brute, aren't I?'

'You said it.'

'But when you get to know me better——'

'I've no desire to know you better, Mr Vance,' she retorted.

He ignored her rudeness. 'You'll discover that I do have very strong feelings on some subjects. And let me tell you, if you persist in treating me like a bull to be baited, there's a distinct possibility that you'll get more than you bargained for.'

She shot him a defiant look. 'I'm not afraid,' she said, but inwardly she felt a sudden frisson of pure terror. She was out of her depth with this man, however much she refused to acknowledge it. Bull-baiting—it was not a bad piece of description, except in what she knew of the sport, the odds were on the baiters, not the bull. This man was more than just a tough male animal, assured and confident of his own powers. He was crafty as well. Up till now he had been playing with her, she knew. If it came to a serious battle of wits, she had a strong suspicion that she would be on the losing side and she didn't like the idea.

'I'm glad to hear it,' he told her pleasantly. 'It should

make life round here quite interesting, even if you do
capitulate in the end.'

'Who's talking about capitulation?' she asked him
pertly.

'I am.'

He could move quickly, she knew that. But, even so,
he took her by surprise so completely that she had no
time to react. One arm was around her before she knew
what was happening and his hand had caught hers and
was pinning them powerlessly behind her, while the
other jerked her still closer to him.

She trembled with a sudden strange excitement.
There was something about this man that set her senses
alight in a way that was new to her.

'I warned you,' he said tautly. 'And you wouldn't
listen to me, would you? You thought you knew better.
Well, if reasoning with you doesn't work, let's see if
this method brings any better results.'

His mouth came down on hers with an insistence
that she could not escape. And, after a few seconds of
heart-stopping sensation, she was not sure that she
even felt like trying to evade him. Her lips parted instinctively under his, her untutored senses began to
respond to the skilled assault he was making on them.
She must not surrender to him; that would be too
humiliating. But she was not listening to any warnings
now. It was too late for that, and she was being carried
along by a tide of pleasure.

Until he released her abruptly and stood back from
her, leaving her half dizzy at the suddenness of his
action. 'Perhaps that is the way to deal with you,' he
said musingly. 'It shuts you up, at least. You haven't
had much experience of men, have you, Verity?'

At a sheltered convent school it was hardly likely that
she would have done, but she didn't tell him that.

Instead she shrugged. 'Did you expect me to respond with enthusiasm? I'm not one of your women. *I* don't even like you!'

She did not like the smile that he gave her either. 'I didn't find you lacking in enthusiasm, just expertise.'

'Oh, you—you——'

'Yes?'

She could not think of a word insulting enough to describe him. Her hand itched to make contact with his face, but she knew that if she tried anything of the kind he would take punitive action—and she had already had one taste of his mastery of her in that department. Instead she wiped her hand across her lips in a way that was intended to leave no doubt in his mind about how repellent she had found his kiss.

'Just keep away from me, Mr Vance,' she warned as she backed cautiously towards the door.

'You'd better make it Ramón,' he said carelessly. A devil danced in his eyes. 'As we're on kissing terms.'

'That was the first and last kiss you'll get from me!'

'A pity. With a little practice you could be quite something.'

'So could you. You might start by trying to learn a few manners,' Verity flung at him. Then she took to her heels and fled to the safety of her own room, locking the door behind her as if she feared his pursuit. She need not have worried. The corridor outside her room remained silent and she was able to breathe again.

Verity burned all over at the thought of that episode. How could he have acted like that? More important, how could *she*? Was it really Verity Williams who had said those things, who had provoked a man to that pitch and who had enjoyed—yes, enjoyed what had followed? What was it about Ramón Vance that stirred her up like this?

Her father had noticed it and had confronted her after the meal when she had withdrawn to the kitchen to make coffee. She intended to leave the two men to talk business while she washed up the dishes and then retired to her room.

'What's the matter with you, Verity?' Mark Williams followed her out of the dining-room, shutting the door behind him so that their visitor could not hear the exchange.

She feigned ignorance. 'Wasn't the meal all right? I did my best.'

And she had, too. She had been determined to show the arrogant Mr Vance that there was one area in which she rated reasonably highly, even by his standards. *Empanadas*, small pasties containing a mixture of meat, raisins and olives, had been followed by *arroz con pollo*, one of her father's favourite dishes, consisting of rice, chicken, eggs and vegetables in a spicy, savoury sauce. She had offered cheese and biscuits for dessert. Neither she nor her father favoured the sweet, sticky pastries that were the usual fare on Argentinian tables. If their guest had the traditional sweet tooth of his countrymen, it was just too bad, she thought.

'The food was excellent and you know it. I'm talking about the way you acted.'

'What about it?' she asked, although she knew precisely what he meant.

'Verity, I was ashamed of you. You hardly spoke to Mr. Vance unless you had to, and even then you acted like a spoilt child. I don't know what he must be thinking of you!'

She had a fair idea. After all, he had abused her in round enough terms before dinner. She felt herself go hot at the memory of that dialogue. 'Does it matter?'

she said defiantly. 'Come on, Dad. He's no fool, I'll give him that. He knows that he's not welcome here.'

'It's a difficult position to be in and I'm sure he accepts that. But you aren't helping. If you're behaving like this out of some sense of loyalty to me, forget it, love.'

'I just don't like the man.'

'You don't like him? Don't be stupid! You've hardly met him. How can you possibly tell whether you like the man or not? He seems pleasant enough to me.'

Verity shrugged. She knew that she was not helping matters. 'I'm sorry, Dad, really I am. I can't help it. I suppose it's just instant antipathy. It happens sometimes.'

'Well, it's not going to happen now,' her father said with unexpected firmness. 'Too much hangs on this man's say-so for us to be deliberately making an enemy of him.'

'Don't ask me to play the hypocrite and act as if I liked him, she begged, 'I couldn't do it.'

'I'm not expecting you to do anything of the sort. But I am telling you to treat him with the common courtesy that you'd give to any guest in the house.' Mark Williams sighed heavily. 'Don't make things any harder for me, Verity, please. He'll be here for a while, looking round at everything. It's not exactly going to be a bed of roses for me, you know, having to take him round with me all the time, having him watch me critically at every turn. If you're going to antagonise the man in the evenings, life isn't going to be very happy for any of us in the next few weeks.'

'The next few weeks?' Verity echoed. 'He'll be here that long?'

'Apparently.'

She had groaned at the thought. How could she bear

his presence in the house for a few days, let alone for an extended stay? But she had to try. 'I'll do my best, Dad,' she told him. 'But don't expect miracles, will you?'

'That's my girl!' he smiled, and had returned to the dining-room looking considerably relieved.

Their guest noticed her sudden efforts to be pleasant to him. Verity could tell from the gleam of faint amusement in the dark glance that slanted across at her all too frequently, although the bulk of his remarks were directed at her father. So he found it funny, seeing her forced to crawl to him, did he?

After a quick cup of coffee she had excused herself to wash the dishes, leaving the two men to talk business. Ramón Vance thanked her for the meal, complimenting her on her cooking, and she accepted the praise with a bright, false smile that she was sure hadn't deceived him for a moment. Hostilities were only postponed between them, something told her that.

Verity sighed heavily as she pushed aside the covers and got out of bed. The very thought of Ramón Vance had spoilt the day for her already. And every day in the immediate future would be ruined for as long as *he* chose to stay at Vista Hermosa. But if her father could stick it, so could she, she resolved. She glanced at her watch and frowned. Here she was daydreaming and it was nearly half-past six! She would be late with breakfast if she didn't hurry. Her father was generally up at dawn and he would be getting impatient, although she doubted if their visitor would rise this early. In Buenos Aires they followed European customs and businessmen did not have to be in their offices until nine o'clock in the morning.

He proved her wrong, of course. *He* would, she thought resentfully, as washed and dressed in working gear of slacks and a cotton T-shirt, she made her way to the kitchen.

'*Buenos dias, señorita*,' he greeted her from the doorway as she was busying herself getting out plates from a cupboard. She jumped, and, only by clutching the crockery frantically to her, avoided disaster.

She recovered and put the plates down on the table. '*Buenos dias*,' she responded stiffly.

He looked pointedly at his watch. 'Your father said that you were usually up before now. I was wondering if you'd overslept.'

'Were you going to come and shake me out of bed?' she asked him.

'I was giving you another five minutes,' he said calmly. 'And then, who knows? Desperate diseases require desperate remedies.'

'And are you desperate for my company, Mr Vance?'

'No,' he said shortly. 'Just for breakfast. I've a hard day ahead of me.'

'So I see. You've certainly dressed the part,' she told him scathingly. 'Are you proposing to show the *gauchos* a thing or two?'

His business suit of the previous day had been discarded in favour of a casually-buttoned denim shirt, revealing the tanned column of his throat. Jeans of the same material hugged his hips and strong-muscled thighs and were belted with a stout leather strap, clasped with an ornate silver buckle. There was not much of the city-slicker about him this morning, she had to admit. He looked lean, tough and dangerous. But looks were not enough on the *pampas*. A man had to prove himself a man. Appearances counted for little or nothing: action was all.

He was not going to rise to the bait. 'We'll see,' he

said carelessly. 'After breakfast, if it's ever forthcoming.'

Verity scowled at him and got on with her preparations. The sooner they ate, the sooner the obnoxious man would be out of the house and out of her presence. In record time she served up the usual meal of *bife a caballo*, steak topped with two fried eggs, with mountains of toast and coffee. She ate little herself, but the two men made a hearty breakfast. Her father at least would need the energy for the morning ahead. Coaxing frightened animals through the dipping troughs was hard, back-breaking work.

Verity smiled to herself as she watched the two figures walk down the track from the house. Ramón Vance topped her father by a good six inches and carried himself with a powerful vigour that was missing in the other man. But she knew which one the *gauchos* would listen to and obey. Her father had always worked on the principle of never asking a hired hand to do something that he could not perform adequately himself, and his men respected him for it.

'A *gaucho* always retains that fierce independence of his, even when he's up for hire,' her father had told her once. 'You have to earn his loyalty and trust. And they're not given lightly.'

She could believe that. She knew the half dozen or so men who rode with her father daily. Most of them had been at Vista Hermosa since before she had been born. They were men of few words, ill at ease in unfamiliar company, but quite capable of spotting the sham or the phoney that they might encounter there. They certainly would not be under any delusions when it came to judging Ramón Vance. He would never know that he had been put on trial. There were any number of subtle ways of testing his worth. But they would have his true measure in the end, and then heaven help him if he expected any co-operation!

It would serve him right for butting in where he was not wanted, Verity thought with some satisfaction. There would be trouble if he decided to replace her father with another man, and it was as well for him to realise the fact. She tidied up the breakfast dishes and set about her morning's housework almost cheerfully. Perhaps, when Ramón Vance saw the enormity of the task that he had taken on, he would lose a little of that high-and-mighty attitude that he had adopted.

The men broke early in the afternoon for lunch and a rest from the heat of the sun. If Mark Williams was in the distant pastures he usually took something to eat with him or joined his men in one of their campfire roasts, but when he was near the house Verity took him a basket of food. It made a break for both of them to share an hour or so together.

Nothing had been said about returning to the house for lunch, so she assumed that today there would be no variation in the custom. Accordingly she packed a mound of sandwiches, cheese and fruit, and unloaded a pack of beer bottles from the fridge where they were nicely chilled. After a hard morning's work her father would be ready for that and she supposed Ramón Vance would be the same. Even supermen had to refuel occasionally, she thought sourly.

The heat hit her in a solid wall as she shouldered the basket and made her way down the drive to the dipping troughs. It must be nearly a hundred degrees today, hot even for January, the peak of the summer months. Even the breeze that was a constant attractive feature of *pampas* life felt as if it was burning her skin and Verity could feel the trickle of perspiration down her back and between her breasts as she plodded on. It was not far, only a twenty-minute walk, but she felt as if she had been put through a wringer by the time her goal was in sight.

'*Vaca, vaca!*' She could hear the men shouting encouragement to the terrified cattle as she got nearer. The frequent dipping was necessary to keep the animals disease-free and comfortable, but the poor beasts never realised that and did everything they could to avoid the process as the men released them from the pens where they had been confined overnight and herded them with the aid of dogs towards the first of the troughs. The stench of cattle was almost overpowering in this heat, although Verity was used to it, and she wrinkled her nose distastefully.

The first of the herd was out of the wooden stockade now and being driven towards the steep stone trough and the rest were following. The sleek black bodies gleamed in the sunlight as they emerged damply at the far end of the troughs and were bunched together again, ready for the drive back to the pastures from which they had come.

Verity paused, well out of the way of the action. She had been around this sort of operation long enough to know of the dangers that could be encountered by the unwary. A hoof lashing out could knock a man unconscious and his chances of survival were nil if he was unlucky enough to fall in the path of frightened, skittish cattle. She stopped by the fence, admiring for the umpteenth time the skill with which the *gauchos* moved the beasts in their charge. Man and horse were as one as they wheeled and turned around the shifting cattle, urging, pushing and cajoling to gain their objective. Their dogs would not win any prizes for good looks. Most of them were cross-bred animals of bizarre appearance. But they too were a vital part of the team as they ran round the outside of the herd, keeping away from the dangerous hooves, but ensuring that the beasts were kept in line.

Verity glanced over to where Ramón Vance was standing with her father by the entrance to the troughs. She wondered what he was making of it all. Even a complete ignoramus about ranch life ought to be able to appreciate a display of skill like this. There was not much he could find fault with here. Her lip curled slightly as she studied him. He was still trying to look the part, she thought, as she noted the long stockman's whip that rested in one lean hand.

As if aware of her scrutiny he looked suddenly away from the animals and straight across at her. The brown eyes held hers for a long moment, almost as if he could read what was in her mind, and she was the first to look away. Damn the man, did he have to bare her innermost thoughts every time he gazed at her? Verity fought for composure. Any moment now, when the last of this batch was through, they would call a halt, then she would have to go and greet the man as if she liked him. She would have to pretend, although she knew that she wouldn't be fooling anyone except her father. Ramón Vance had her measure all too clearly. But perhaps, if he saw that she was trying to be pleasant in spite of everything, he would give her father a fair hearing. That was the main thing, after all.

The last two bulky black bodies struggled through the troughs and stumbled out at the far end to be driven with the rest of the cattle into the far pen. It had been a good morning's work, Verity could tell. There were so often delays while fugitive cows were rounded up again to join the herd. Obviously nothing like that had happened today. Her father would be relieved; he wanted to make a good showing. She saw him raise a hand and heard the call to stop work. She picked up the basket and, waving to attract his attention, headed towards him across the now empty pen.

The cattle had kicked up a fair amount of dust in their to-ings and fro-ings. If it hadn't been for that Verity was sure that she would have seen the danger and taken avoidance action. As it was the first notion she had of any trouble was almost too late. She was only aware of a coiled brown body, the same shade as the ground, and of a head rearing up to strike at her. Somebody screamed and she heard the noise as from a distance, although it had come from her own throat.

'*Culebra!*' one of the *gauchos* shouted a warning. '*Cuidado, niña! Culebra!*' He moved towards her in an attempt to help her, but he was a hundred yards away.

She stood as if paralysed, waiting for the attack. But it never came. The thong of a whip, moving as swiftly and as menacingly as the reptile itself, circled through the air. One moment the snake had been poised to strike, the next it was writhing in the dust, and she herself had been seized in a strong hold and whirled out of danger.

'You little fool,' a voice muttered in her ear. 'Can't you look where you're going?'

With an effort she turned to face her rescuer. In the background she was vaguely aware of one of the men dealing a death blow to the snake and saw the still twisting body being unceremoniously tossed away. 'Was it poisonous?' she asked.

'It could have given you a nasty bite, I imagine,' Ramón Vance told her. 'Enough to put even you out of action for a while.'

'I just didn't see it,' she said stupidly. Now that the danger was over, she felt suddenly weak with reaction. It had all happened so quickly. Her legs buckled beneath her, but before she could fall he had caught her and was holding her in a none too gentle grasp.

'You're not going to faint,' he commanded her. 'Come on now, Verity, pull yourself together. The danger's over now.'

She knew that, but somehow she could still not quite take in what had happened. She wanted to do nothing more than burst into floods of tears, but his words had a bracing effect on her and stopped her in time. She leant gratefully against him, taking strength from the unyielding firmness of his body. Then, responding automatically to the order that he had snapped out at her, she braced herself and stood up by her own efforts.

'Verity, are you all right?' Her father was with them now, his face pale with shock. 'It didn't touch you, did it?'

'No,' she reassured him quickly. 'It didn't have a chance, even though I nearly trod on it, it was so near me. Whoever sent that whip flying over was too quick for it.'

'Thank God for that! That was a magnificent throw, Vance.' Her father turned to the other man, congratulating him. 'Where did you learn to do that? Did you train with the circus?'

He shrugged. 'It was a lucky throw, that's all. Any of the others could have managed it if they'd been within range. It just happened that they weren't and I was. No great hero stuff.'

'You? You saved me?' Verity asked him incredulously. 'But how on earth——'

'Just as well that I dressed the part, wasn't it?' There was a faint edge to his voice as he cast her words of that morning back at her. 'Excuse me, will you? I want to talk to the men. Oh, and Williams——'

'Yes?'

'Go easy with her, will you? I should take her back to the house. She's had a bit of a shake-up, one way and another. It'll take a while to pick up the pieces.' And, with a curt nod, he strode away to where a group of the men were standing, obviously discussing the incident.

'Come on, young lady, back to the house with you. Can you walk?'

'Yes, I'm all right, Dad. Don't make a fuss. I'm fine, really I am. All I need is——'

'All you need is a lie-down. Vance was right—you've had a shock.'

Still protesting weakly, Verity allowed him to guide her towards the path down which she had only just come. Her knees felt strange and jelly-like and her head was spinning. She must not faint; *he* had told her not to. But suddenly the ground was coming up to meet her in waves, rising and falling in a totally unpredictable way. Before blackness engulfed her she thought she heard Ramón Vance's voice. But whatever he was saying passed her by as she collapsed into grateful oblivion.

CHAPTER FOUR

He was still there telling her off when Verity awoke. At first she thought that she was asleep and dreaming. How else could she be undressed and in bed in her own room with the afternoon sun still high in the sky? Then she remembered.

'I told you you weren't going to faint,' Ramón Vance said accusingly. He was sitting in a chair by her bedside and his powerful frame dominated the whole room.

'It looks as if you were proved wrong for once,' she said weakly. 'What are you doing here?'

'Playing nursemaid to you.' A glint in his eyes told her that he wasn't particularly enjoying the experience.

'Oh.' She registered the information rather blankly. Her head still felt fuzzy and her brain did not seem to be functioning too well at the moment. 'Where's Dad?'

'He's gone back to work.'

'But I want him,' she said childishly, before she could stop herself.

'Too bad. He's got more important things to do than soothing your fevered brow.'

'You sent him back, didn't you?' she accused him. 'He didn't want to leave me.'

'He was a bit worried about you. You went out like a light and it scared him, but I told him there was no need to worry.'

'That would set his mind at rest instantly, of course.'

'Of course,' he agreed. 'Particularly as I offered to stay with you to make sure that you were all right.'

'And am I? Tell me, doctor.'

'You seem to be recovering fast,' he said dryly. He took her wrist, the touch of his long, well-kept fingers cool against her skin, and Verity felt her senses quicken involuntarily. 'Your pulse is still rather unsteady.'

What else did he expect? 'You don't have a very calming effect on me,' she told him. 'In fact, you make my blood boil most of the time.'

'Apparently so. I can't do anything right where you're concerned, can I?' He did not sound as if it bothered him too much.

'Not much,' she said, and then remembered. 'I'm sorry, I haven't thanked you for rescuing me.'

'I wondered if you'd get round to it.'

He did not make easy. 'I'm very grateful.' The words came out stiffly, reluctantly.

'Don't force yourself,' he said drily. 'I'll survive without pretty speeches, if you find them that hard to deliver. Yet another part of your education that they neglected at finishing school?'

'I'm not very good at saying thank you to people.' It was the best that she could do by way of apology. 'Besides, how *do* you thank someone for maybe saving your life? It sounds so melodramatic, even if it's true.'

He laughed softly. 'Ah yes—the famous English dislike of embarrassing people. You needn't worry about sparing my feelings, Verity. I'm not one of your stiff-lipped Englishmen,' he told her mockingly. 'It would take a lot to make me blush.'

She could well imagine it. How many men would be sitting, as he was doing, in a strange female's bedroom, completely at his ease and chatting as if he did this sort of thing every day? For all she knew to the contrary, perhaps he did. They were sophisticated folk in Buenos Aires.

He had not finished tormenting her yet. 'Of course, if you feel that mere words cannot express your thanks, you could try actions,' he told her wickedly. 'Proverbially, they speak louder, you know.'

'Yes, I suppose I could,' she agreed, striving to match his casual tone.

'But you're not going to, are you?'

'Don't tell me you're disappointed,' she jeered. 'Do you prize my kisses so highly?'

'They have a certain rarity value. But I'll get by without them,' he said smoothly. He studied her for a moment, the dark gaze so penetrating that she shifted uneasily under it. 'What would it take, I wonder, to make you lose your head over a man?'

'More than you've got to offer!'

'Don't make rash statements, Verity,' he told her, 'or I might be tempted to prove to you exactly how wrong they are.'

'Is that a threat or a promise?' she provoked him daringly. What was it about this man that made her throw caution to the winds? It was exciting crossing swords with him, inviting a danger that she had never dreamed of enjoying before.

'Call it a statement of intention,' he said. 'And, in the meantime, here's something on account, just to register my interest.'

He leaned forward, his arms sliding around her and gathering her to him, his movements practised and assured. Ramón Vance was no amateur in the bedroom. His lips burned a sensuous trail of kisses along her bare neck, brushing lightly over her cheek before reaching her mouth. Involuntarily, her lips parted under his as gently, persuasively, he coaxed a response from her.

It was madness and she knew it. But she didn't care. Her arms moved to embrace him, pulling him closer to her, scenting the tangy smell of his cologne as she did so. She had never been this close to a man before, but age-old instinct guided her as she moved a hand to caress the springy softness of his dark hair. Strange sensations were pulsing through her, making her aware of appetites that she had never known before. What was happening to her?

Her whole body was alive now, like a stringed instrument responding to the touch of a skilful player. She made no resistance as Ramón pushed her back against the pillows and moved to cover her with his own body. Her nightdress was pushed aside and he was caressing her, arousing her to a peak of desire that cried out for the satisfaction that only he could bring her.

'Well, does that demonstrate anything to you?' His voice sounded in her ears as if from a long way away. Suddenly he had moved away from her. Seconds before it had seemed that nothing could come between them and the ultimate shared experience. Now he was getting to his feet as if what had happened had been nothing to him.

Disillusion flooded through her. 'You swine!'

'Why? Because I nearly took what you were offering me so eagerly?' A careless hand restored the tousled hair to order and did up the shirt buttons that her questing fingers had prised apart only instants before. 'Or are you cross because I called a halt just as things were getting to an interesting stage?'

'How dare you suggest that I was—that I would——' She floundered in an attempt to express her indignation.

'That you wanted me to make love to you?' he suggested smoothly. 'I think it was a fair conclusion to draw from the way you behaved towards me. I didn't notice you trying to fight me off.'

Verity was silent, ashamed of herself. Then she rallied. 'You took advantage of me,' she accused him. 'No decent man would have behaved the way you did!'

'Wouldn't he just? You don't know much about men, decent or otherwise, if you really believe that. Just thank your stars that you got off so lightly. Next time you may not be so lucky.'

'There won't be a next time,' she vowed.

'We'll see about that,' he shrugged. He tucked the flap of his shirt into the band of his jeans and walked towards the door.

'If you lay a finger on me again, I'll tell my father,' she warned him.

He paused. 'Am I supposed to tremble at the thought? What do you expect your father to do about it? Tackle me with a stockwhip? Can you see me letting him, even if he was foolish enough to try, which I very much doubt? Grow up, Verity. You keep telling me you're not a child any more and you've just done your level best to prove it.' His eyes rested mockingly on the rumpled bed-cover. 'Being an adult means standing on your own feet, not running to Daddy for help every time something doesn't go according to your own little plans.'

'You think you know it all, don't you?' she muttered with loathing in her voice.

'Pretty well,' he agreed. 'So you know where to come if you need any more help in furthering that neglected education of yours.'

'Get out! Get out of my room,' she shouted. 'And get out of my sight!'

'The way you're looking at the moment, it'll be a pleasure. I promised your father I'd stay with you until you were feeling more like your normal self. I think you're restored to your usual bad temper, aren't you? I'll reassure him on that point when I see him.' Ramón opened the door and prepared to leave. 'Oh, and don't bother about a meal tonight. Your father and I will be eating in town. He's promised to introduce me to a couple of people and it'll be more convenient to talk business over a meal.'

'And what am I supposed to do?' she demanded. 'While you're out enjoying yourselves?'

'Cool your heels, I should think. There won't be anyone to listen to that sharp tongue of yours. We won't be late back, but don't pace the floor, will you? I think I've had quite enough of your charming company for one day.'

'The feeling's mutual, believe me. I wouldn't wait up for you if you were the last man on earth!' she raged.

He laughed. 'Fine words, Verity. Take care I don't make you eat them one of these days.' And with that the door shut behind him and she heard his footsteps going away.

'Oh, you—you——' She could not find words bad enough to describe him. Instead she punched her pillow hard, wishing that it could have been his arrogant head. One day, she vowed, she would get even with Ramón Vance for all she had suffered at his hands. She lay back and dreamed of that time, a slow smile curving her lips.

She must have fallen asleep because a glance at her bedside clock showed her that it was nearly six when she roused herself again and thought about getting up. Emotional upsets took more out of one than she realised before, although she would have been hard put to it to decide whether it was the encounter with the snake or the later tussle with Ramón Vance that had left her feeling so tired and drained.

She was hungry—she remembered that she had not had any lunch. Perhaps she would get up and find herself something to eat. She stretched reluctantly, preparing to get out of bed, then crouched back among the bedclothes, clutching them to her in a defensive attitude as a knock came at the door and it opened before she had a chance to ask who was there.

She relaxed when she saw that her visitor was her father, her convulsive grasp of the sheet slackening with relief. So that was what a bout with Ramón Vance did to her!

'How are you feeling, love?' Mark Williams looked anxious. 'Vance and I are due to meet some cattle men in Campo Verde, but I'll cry off, if you don't want to be left on your own.'

'You'll do nothing of the kind,' she told him firmly. 'I'm fine. Anyone would imagine that snake had actually taken a bite out of me instead of just scaring me rigid!'

'It might so easily have done,' her father said soberly. 'I shudder to think what might have happened if Vance hadn't acted so quickly. He was wonderful——'

'Yes, marvellous,' Verity cut him short. She had had enough of Ramón Vance's quick actions to last her a lifetime, and to hear her father singing his praises was more than she could take at the moment.

'I hope you thanked him.'

'Oh, yes,' she assured him, wondering what her father would say if he knew exactly what form those thanks had taken. Ramón Vance's shining armour might be a little tarnished if he did.

'He's a kind man, Verity. And thoughtful. He knew I was needed back with the men, and he insisted on staying with you to set my mind at rest.'

'Really?' She was sceptical. She could not imagine Ramón Vance doing anything that did not suit his own purposes in some way.

'So, after we'd got you to bed, I left you in his hands. He's trained in first-aid, apparently. He——'

'After you what?' Verity jerked upright. 'You're not telling me that Ramón Vance undressed me, are you?' She would never be able to face the man again if she knew *that*!

'Such outraged virtue!' Her father was laughing at her. He would laugh on the other side of his face if he knew the whole story. 'Relax, will you? He carried you up here, dumped you on the bed and left the rest to me. Satisfied?'

Her cheeks were flaming. At least she had been spared the worst indignity. 'Sorry,' she mumbled. 'I thought that—— Well, I'm not a little girl any more and——'

'And I'm as aware of that as anyone.' Mark Williams was amused. 'And I'm only your poor old dad. I don't think it's escaped our guest either. He was giving you quite a few looks over the breakfast table.'

'He wasn't dazzled by my beauty, that's for sure,' she said lightly. 'I expect he was intrigued. He's probably never seen a woman brought up on the *pampas* before and was surprised to find that I didn't actually have straw in my hair and eat with my fingers.'

'Hardly that. He was telling me that he was brought up not far from here. His father had an *estancia* this side of Rosario.'

Hence his skill with the stockwhip, she supposed. She ought to be thankful for that skill. She probably owed her life—or at least her health—to it. 'It's a great pity that he didn't stay there,' she said peevishly. 'He wouldn't be bothering us if he had.'

'If it hadn't been him, it would have been someone else. And maybe someone a good deal worse.'

Impossible, she thought, but she did not say it. 'He seems to have won you over,' she commented.

'I like what I've seen of him so far. He knows what he's doing. He's straight, Verity, a man to trust. I'll get a fair deal from him, I'm sure.'

'You mean it's going to be all right? We can stay?' she asked eagerly. 'Did he say so?' At that moment she was ready to forgive the man almost anything.

'No. It's too soon yet for him to say anything and I wouldn't expect him to. He's looking at everything and weighing it up. He wants to know all the facts. He'll tell me what he's decided when he's good and ready, and I think enough of him to accept his conclusions.'

'Even if he kicks us out?'

'Yes, even if it means that.' Her father frowned. 'He's not a man to do that lightly. I'll abide by what he says.'

'Well, I won't,' Verity said firmly. 'He'll have to carry me off this property feet first if he wants me to go.'

'Let's hope it doesn't come to that, then.' Mark Williams was not going to argue with her. 'Although I'm sure he's got more persuasive methods of dealing with recalcitrant females that he may encounter.'

Except that he had probably never needed to use them until now, Verity thought grimly. 'He likes his women to be sweet and submissive,' she said.

Her father's smile was indulgent. 'And what would

you know about that? Did he tell you so?'

'Not in so many words.' She shrugged. 'But he looks the type, that's all—as if he expects everyone to jump when he gives the word.'

'And that's what I'm going to have to do right now.' Mark Williams consulted his watch. 'We were due to leave five minutes ago. Are you sure you'll be all right, love?'

'For the last time of asking, Dad, yes. Now run along and don't keep the nice man waiting.'

'Minx,' he said fondly, laughing as he went.

Verity got up, dressed and made herself some supper. For all her hunger she did not really feel like eating. She pushed her plate aside before the food was half finished. After she had cleared away the dishes that she had used and washed them up, she wandered back into the living room and paced up and down, strangely restless.

This would not do. It was not like her. There were any number of things waiting to be done when she had a spare moment, and now that it had arrived she did not want to tackle any of them. There was a pile of mending: her father would be going barefoot if she did not darn some of his socks soon. There was that dress that she was halfway to finishing. And, if sewing palled, there was always lots of cleaning to be done. Ramón Vance had made it quite clear what he thought of her attention to that department of the house.

She walked over to the radio and switched it on. It seemed to be a programme in homage to Jorge Borges, Argentina's celebrated literary genius. Verity listened for a few minutes and then, suddenly bored, turned it off. She went to the window and peered out into the pitch darkness of the *pampas* night. There was no sign of life except the whirr of insects and the gentle croaking of the little green frogs that inhabited what had once been a delightful lily pond not far from the house.

She gave a quick, impatient sigh. What was wrong with her tonight? She kept posing the question, although she knew the answer perfectly well. She did not want to think about her first encounter with physical passion, her first real contact with a man. There had been boys whom she had met at the carefully chaperoned, rather decorous gatherings that the nuns had held so that their pupils could be accustomed to the outside world. But the blushing, uncertain adolescents that she had dealt with easily were on a different planet from the man that had kissed her today.

And it had not just been a kiss. Verity's flesh tingled at the memory of the sensations his hands had aroused as they had roamed over her body with unlicensed freedom. Instead of fighting him off she had encouraged him, her response showing him exactly what pleasure he was giving her. It was *he* who had called a halt, not her. He could have done as he pleased with her and she would have let him without resistance. She burned with shame now as she remembered it all, dwelling on every detail. How could she have done it?

She picked up the latest detective story that she had bought last week and had not had time to read until now. It was by one of her favourite authors. She curled up in a chair and opened the book firmly. There was no point in brooding. Ramón Vance would no doubt have dismissed the episode from his mind, and she must too. If only it was not such an effort to forget what had happened between them. She focussed determinedly on Chapter One and started reading.

She partly succeeded. It was an interesting story and the characters were well drawn. But the murderer, a

man with a cast-iron alibi, revealed his hand too soon
and Verity found her attention beginning to wander.
She caught herself straining for the sound of the car
that would signal the two men's return to the *estancia*.
Twice she jumped up, thinking that she saw the head-
lights of the ranch Land Rover coming along the
drive.

She was being stupid, she told herself. If she had
any sense she would be safely out of the way when
they got back. After all, Ramón Vance had as good as
ordered her from his sight for the rest of the day, and
she had grave doubts as to her ability to greet him
with any degree of normality in front of her father.
She was sure that something would reveal her shameful
behaviour, however hard she tried to act naturally. But
why should she hide herself away? It was *his* fault, just
as much as hers, she thought rebelliously, sitting down
and taking up the book again.

At ten o'clock, however, discretion got the better of
valour and she went to her room and got ready for
bed. But not for sleep. She lay back against her pillows,
her head tossing restlessly from one side to another as
the thoughts ran around her head. For the first time it
occurred to her to wonder who Ramón Vance and her
father were meeting. Cattle men, her father had said.
Dealers? Buyers? Financiers? No doubt she would discover in the morning. Still listening for the sound of
the car, she slid into a troubled sleep.

She learned next day from her father that their
dinner guests had been from neighbouring *estancias*,
Señor Fernando Delgado from the enormously pros-
perous Los Molinos which lay to the east of Vista
Hermosa and Señor Manuel Castillo who farmed to
the north. Verity knew them both, although she pre-
ferred the jovial Señor Castillo, who had always made

a fuss of her when she was a child and who had never been too busy to sit her on his knee and tell her stories about *gauchos* and their folklore.

It was funny how Señor Castillo who had no children and whose wife had died young was so much more approachable than the rather snobbish Señor Delgado who had three children, all daughters. His eldest child, Isabel, had been two years ahead of Verity at school. She shared her father's condescending attitude to those she considered her inferiors. She also shared his dark, rather saturnine features and his thin, slightly aquiline nose.

'Why on earth did you have to eat in town?' Verity asked in surprise. 'We know them. They've been over here before. It's not as if they were total strangers to be entertained at the best restaurant.' She frowned. 'I could have cooked you——'

'After a fright like you had yesterday, you weren't in a condition to cook anything, and we'd no intention of asking you to.'

'You mean Mr Vance had no intention,' she said coldly. It was strange how she always accorded him that English title, as if he was indeed the old, rather fussy Anglo-Argentinian that she had first imagined him. 'I suppose my cooking's not up to his standards, is that it?'

'There's no need to fly off the handle, love,' her father rebuked her gently. 'I'm sure he didn't mean any slight to you. But we were talking business and you would have been bored to tears, you know. It was much more convenient doing it the way we did. And you didn't have any washing up to do either.'

Why argue? It was not worth it. Verity let the matter drop and asked instead why the meeting had been arranged. 'I don't suppose Ramón Vance would fix something like that without some ulterior motive?' she enquired sourly.

Mark Williams laughed. 'He's an astute man, Verity. He wanted confirmation of the local picture that I'd given him and to talk about the problems that they'd been encountering on their own ranches. He wanted them to come clean about their affairs without giving away too much of ours. Not that they don't know a fair amount of my troubles by now.'

She grinned. 'Señor Delgado's as close as a clam. I bet he gave you a hard time!' She relished the prospect of their arrogant visitor trying in vain to obtain the information he wanted. 'Was it heavy going?'

'Not a bit of it. Ten minutes into dinner and he and Vance were as thick as thieves. I've never seen anything like it. I heard more about the inside workings of Los Molinos than I've gleaned in twenty years. And Castillo was lapping it up too. I tell you, Verity, that man's a marvell!'

'At pulling wool over people's eyes, perhaps.' Verity was unconvinced. She knew what the man was really like and was not going to change her opinion.

But it seemed that she was out on a limb where her judgment of Ramón Vance was concerned. As the days went by it became increasingly apparent that the new-comer was charming everyone. His visit to Campo Verde had set female hearts fluttering all over the town, as those who had actually seen him communicated the news of his dark good looks, his breadth of shoulder and air of command to those who had had the misfor-tune to miss them in the flesh. Any stranger in town aroused interest, but this one was causing more than the usual stir.

'*Que hombre!*' Maria Lopez, who owned the largest store in town and who had supplied goods to Vista

Hermosa since before Verity was born, enthused over the handsome Señor Vance, the pleasant Señor Vance, the gallant Señor Vance, who had come into her shop and talked to her with as much deference as he would have given to the President's wife. 'And me in my old working apron, *niña*, with stains down the front. Such a man!' Her shrewd, button black eyes glinted craftily as she looked at Verity. '*Y soltero tambien!* There's a chance for you to get a fine husband there, *chica*, if you make a set at him.'

'I'm not in the market for a husband,' Verity said coldly. 'He can stay a bachelor for all I care. I'm certainly not interested.'

'Rubbish! Every woman is interested in a man like that. She cannot help but be.'

'So it seems. Everyone I meet wants to know about him. Let's hope it's a nine days' wonder. Maybe a circus will come to town and we'll have something else to talk about. That's one subject that I'm heartily sick of.'

Maria chuckled. 'So you don't like him, eh? Is that what you're trying to tell me?'

'Not much,' Verity said briefly. 'I'll grant you he's good-looking, but he's not my type.'

'We'll see, *niña*. Somehow I don't think you're quite as indifferent as you make out.' And old Maria had laughed until her sides had shaken. '*Que hombre!*'

What a man indeed, Verity thought as she left the store. And it was not just the women who approved of him. He had won over the men too. The *gauchos*, traditionally slow and reserved in their dealings with outsiders, approved of Ramón Vance. He had *machismo*, they said. They admired the ease with which he rode their horses, dealing with the sheepskin saddle and the leather stirrups with consummate skill. They respected the way he could talk to them about cattle and the problems that they encountered with them. They liked the fact that he was able to keep up with the stiff pace they set as he accompanied them about their daily tasks around the *estancia*. Strangely, they did not seem to resent the notes that he took down or his suggestions for improvements about the place. He was a man's man, they told her father admiringly, someone they would willingly trust with their lives if they had to. And that was no mean compliment.

Even her father liked the man. He had respected him from the first, approving of the straight, no-nonsense approach that he took. The episode with the snake had admittedly been a short-cut to Mark Williams' favour, but, if it had not taken place, Verity was sure that it would not have been long before her father had offered his hand in friendship.

Ramón Vance had everyone eating out of his hand. It suited him to play it that way. It made his task easier if he got co-operation. But she was equally certain that he would have gone ahead with his job in the face of opposition. He was that kind of man. He would have bulldozed his way through any kind of barriers set to hinder him. A good man to have on one's side; a bad man to cross.

But he could be sure of one thing: Verity had no intention of joining the chorus of people singing his praises. Let him cajole everyone else into his way of thinking, but he need not think that she had changed her views by one iota. She avoided him as much as possible and took great care never to be alone with him. She did not trust him an inch.

He noticed, of course, although she took pains to conceal her manoeuvres from her father, knowing that it would worry him. At first it seemed to amuse Ramón

Vance that she refused to capitulate, fighting on when all around her had surrendered to him. She was faintly puzzled by his reaction: she had thought that he would see her behaviour as a challenge. It was a relief, she told herself. She did not want any more sparring matches with the man. He was impossible. But, underneath, she admitted to a slight feeling of disappointment that he should have accepted his lack of success with her so readily. A real *man* would not have given up so easily, she argued to herself. Not that it mattered in the least to her. She was totally indifferent. Just let him finish his survey of Vista Hermosa, make up his mind what was to be done there and leave them alone.

'How much longer is he staying?' she asked her father in one of the brief moments that they got alone these days. Their guest was in the stables talking horses with Juan, the man who looked after them.

Her father laughed. He seemed more relaxed than he had been for a while. Verity had the impression that things weren't going too badly. Reprieve had not been officially granted, but she had the feeling that it might be on the way, although, superstitiously, they avoided discussing the subject. 'What's the matter, love?' he asked. 'Is the housework getting you down? I know it's one more person for you to cook and clean for, but you've been managing wonderfully well. Ramón was saying the other day that he'll be running to fat if he eats much more of your good cooking!'

She could not say that she had noticed any evidence of it. His tall frame did not carry an ounce of excess flab. She supposed that the exercise that he was getting ensured that. What did he do in Buenos Aires? she wondered. Perhaps he worked out in one of the numerous gyms that existed for busy executives? It was more likely that his pursuit of women kept him trim. Or did they pursue him?

'I'm all right,' she fended off her father's query. 'A little bored, I suppose. You seem to be tied up all the time. I don't see very much of you.'

'You don't want to spend your time with an old man like me,' he teased her. 'You need some young company. Get Ramón to take you riding. He'd like that, I'm sure.'

'Maybe.' She kept her tone carefully noncommittal. There was no point in telling her father that she would die rather than ask any such thing of Ramón Vance. She did not want his company, in the house or out of it.

'I'll mention it to him,' Mark Williams offered.

'No, there's no need,' she said quickly. 'I can talk to him myself. Really, Dad, anyone would think I was two years old, the way you treat me sometimes!'

'Methuselah,' he teased her and, in the ensuing laughter, the subject they were discussing was forgotten.

CHAPTER FIVE

UNFORTUNATELY for Verity matters did not stay that way. Two days later, as she was washing the breakfast dishes, she had the sudden feeling that she was being watched. She turned to see Ramón Vance in the doorway.

'Did you want something?' she asked distantly. Away from her father's presence she saw no reason to keep up the pleasantly civil tone that she adopted at mealtimes and on the other occasions when she was forced to suffer their visitor's company.

She had not really looked in his direction at breakfast, keeping her eyes on her plate and letting her thoughts rove in other directions as usual. She rarely spoke to him unless directly addressed. Now she noted that his usual working clothes, serviceable jeans topped with a casual shirt, had been replaced by a formal business suit that fitted him superbly. His white shirt emphasised the tan of his face, bronzed by the long hours that he had spent recently in the *pampas* sun. He wore an immaculately knotted silk tie in a discreet shade, and his dark, hand-made shoes gleamed with polish. Clothes did not make the man, Verity reminded herself firmly, resisting an involuntary tug of attraction.

'I have to go to Córdoba on business,' he said. 'Your father tells me that you want a taste of the bright lights. Do you want to come with me?'

If it had been anyone else making the offer, she would have accepted eagerly, not hesitating for a moment. As it was she wavered, then told him, 'No, I don't think so. Thank you anyway.'

A dark brow raised mockingly, he took her up on her refusal. 'Why not? I understood that you were bored to tears with domesticity and craving a little excitement.'

But definitely not the sort that *he* could provide, Verity thought warily. 'I don't choose to go,' she said carefully.

'You mean you don't choose to go with me. Isn't that it?' he asked.

'I've got work to do.' She dodged the question. 'The house needs——'

'I'm well aware of what the house needs. It can wait. A day won't make any difference,' he said crisply. 'Well?'

'I've got to—I must——' Verity's voice tailed off miserably as she tried desperately to find an adequate excuse for not going with him. 'I can't go, that's all.'

'Can't doesn't exist in my vocabulary.' He looked at his watch, then told her, 'You've got half an hour to get yourself ready. I assume that even you will want to try to pretty yourself for a trip to the big city. Go and get ready—I'll meet you by the car.' Having delivered his orders, he prepared to go. Then, catching sight of the expression on her face, he paused. 'Oh, there's just one thing——'

'What?' she asked rudely.

'I don't like being kept waiting. If you're not there on time——'

'You'll go without me,' Verity concluded, faintly relieved. He had just shown her how to escape him. If she did not turn up, he would get impatient and leave on his own, which was exactly what she wanted to happen. 'That would be a pity, wouldn't it?' She gave him a sweet, false smile. 'I'll try not to disappoint you.'

'Will you? I'm glad to hear it,' he said smoothly. 'Because if you're not ready and waiting for me in precisely thirty minutes, I'll have to come and find you. And if you're not dressed by then, I'll help you.'

'You wouldn't dare!' she challenged him.

'Wouldn't I? Don't put me to the test, Verity.' His face was full of mockery. 'You wouldn't be the first, believe me.'

'I'll lock my door.'

He laughed scornfully. 'That wouldn't present too many problems to a determined man,' he told her. 'And you'd be amazed just how determined I can be when someone tries to cross me.'

'I don't want to go to Córdoba with you,' she said angrily, truthful at last.

'Too bad,' he shrugged. 'I'm not interested in what you want. I'm in charge here and I'm telling you what you'll do. Is that understood?'

'I haven't much option, have I?'

'Not much,' he agreed.

She was defeated and she knew it. There was no fighting Ramón Vance in this mood. 'All right, I'll come with you.'

'Not the most gracious acceptance I've ever received from a lady,' he commented lazily.

'I'm not a lady.'

'No, but you might get there some day. *If* you try.' He turned and headed away from her. 'You've rather less than twenty-five minutes to turn yourself into a fair imitation of one,' he called back to her. 'I should get weaving, if I were you. Transformation scenes usually take a bit of effort outside fairy tales.'

'Beast! Arrogant, domineering beast!' Verity

muttered to herself as she kept a hold on her temper with a struggle and forced herself to finish the dishes and leave them to drain. She had no doubt that Ramón Vance meant exactly what he said. She had a quarter of an hour now. She stripped off her apron and ran to her room. One of these days she would get even with that man!

A quick glance at her wardrobe revealed only one possible dress for the outing, and she donned it rapidly. She was not sure if he would find it up to Buenos Aires standards, but for Córdoba it would pass muster. It was a simply cut cotton in a shade of pink that had always flattered her, and it was a dress that always gave her confidence. And, heaven knows, she needed a boost at the moment.

Verity brushed her hair and applied a little make-up. Her eyes in the mirror stared back at her, wide and apprehensive. She was not looking forward to long hours spent in Ramón Vance's company. It was a fair journey to Córdoba, even in a fast car. What on earth would they talk about? Or would he drive in total silence? In a way that would be even worse.

Five minutes left and she was panicking now. Her hand trembled as she tried to apply a coat of lipstick and she had to wipe off her first attempt with a tissue and try again. Damn the man! He had no right to get her worked up like this. There, she was ready, and if he disapproved of the end result it was just too bad. She knew she was no beauty, so why bother trying to pretend? With a final glance in the mirror she slipped her feet into her best navy-blue shoes and headed for the door. She did not want Ramón coming to find her!

She skidded to the front door with seconds to spare from the deadline that he had given her and then slowed to a casual walk that was meant to demonstrate to him, if he was waiting for her outside, that she did not give a fig for his ultimatum. But he had his back turned to her, speaking to one of the men, as she paused on the steps.

'I'm ready!' she called, interrupting the conversation.

He spun round at that and for a second she suffered his critical appraisal of her appearance. Suddenly she was glad that she had made an effort as she saw what could have been a glint of approval in the dark eyes.

'Well, will I do?' she asked pertly. She could tell from the dazzled look on the face of the man beside him that she had made a distinct impression there. But she was not interested in him.

'You'll do.' Ramón Vance opened the car door for her to get in. 'I'll be with you in a minute.' And he turned away again, obviously wanting to finish his conversation.

Verity felt suddenly flat. She supposed that it was too much to expect him to praise her, to appreciate the effort that she had made to look nice. But no; the approving look had clearly been for her obedience, not for her appearance. She wished now that she had worn her shabbiest dress; he would probably not have noticed the difference.

She got into the car and sat there disconsolately. Then she heard a laughing exchange between the two men and Ramón got into the driver's seat, slamming the door behind him. He started the engine and prepared to move off.

'*Adios, Don Ramón, que tenga suerte!*'

'*Adios.*' Her companion waved as they headed down the drive.

Don Ramón indeed! How dared the hired hands accord him that old-fashioned title of respect and treat

him in that way, half deferential, half companionable,
like a well-loved master? In the space of a few weeks
he seemed to have manoeuvred himself into a position
of trust and authority. Why didn't people realise what
he was really like? Was she the only person to see
through the façade to the hard, cold man underneath
who would stop at nothing to gain his own ends?

He seemed in a high good humour all of a sudden,
his lean features relaxed in a way that made him seem
almost human for once. Verity could see why some
women might find him attractive, she conceded to herself. But not her. Suddenly she itched to wipe the smile
off his face.

'Why was Felipe wishing you good luck?' she asked
him. 'Doesn't he think too much of your ability to
handle a car?'

He laughed with genuine amusement. 'I don't think
that was the question at issue.'

'Then what was?' She was puzzled.

He glanced sideways at her, still amused. 'My ability
to handle you. He thought I should make a pass at you
because you were looking attractive.'

'Oh.' Verity wished she hadn't asked. 'He had no right
to suggest anything of the kind,' she said primly.

'Only the right of any man who sees a pretty girl
and admires her. He knew you were out of his league,
so he wished me success with you instead. There's
generosity for you, if you like.'

'I don't like. I'm not a chattel to be handed from
one man to another. This is the twentieth century, in
case you hadn't realised,' she told him coldly.

'I had, but I doubt if Felipe bothers too much about
it. The *gaucho* lives pretty much as he's always done
without making many concessions to modern living. A
woman has her uses, of course. She's there to share his

bed, bear his sons, tend his home when he has one——'

'And take any treatment he hands out to her without complaint. What an attractive picture you paint,' Verity said sarcastically. 'I wonder why I'm not panting to lead such a life.'

'It has its advantages.'

'For the man!'

'Argentina is still a man's country. Accept it. You won't change it, Verity.'

'Perhaps not,' she said stiffly. 'Arguing with someone like you certainly won't get me anywhere, will it?'

He looked slightly impatient. 'Where's your sense of humour?'

'Missing when you're around.'

'I'd noticed. Like you yourself. You're avoiding me these days,' he added.

'What if I am?' she challenged him. 'Aren't you satisfied with the total adoration of everyone else on the *estancia* and outside it? Does it spoil your record to have one person standing aloof?'

'Are you jealous of my success?' he mocked her. 'Would you like lessons on how to win friends and influence people?'

'Do you think I need them?'

He gave a short laugh. If your attitude towards me is anything to go by, you're crying out for a bit of instruction.'

'Thanks for the offer,' she said coldly. 'But no, thanks.'

'You'll regret it.'

'I don't think so.'

Ramón shrugged. 'Please yourself. I imagine you usually do.'

He thought she was selfish and spoilt, and somehow

it hurt her that he should feel that way. Ramón Vance was the first person that she had ever met to inspire such antagonism in her. She almost wished she could explain to him why she acted towards him in a way so alien to her normal nature. But she did not really know the answer herself, and any attempt to excuse her behaviour would only look like weakness. Instead she subsided into silence, staring out of the window at the flat landscape that stretched on every side of them.

For mile after mile the view was unchanging as the road cut through the grassland. Occasionally a patch of thistles or clump of bushes broke the monotony and, equally rarely, a grove of tall trees indicated the presence of a nearby *estancia*. Wire fences showed the boundary limits and on the fence posts, made of hard *quebracho* wood, Verity could see the strange dried mud nests of the *hornero* or ovenbird.

Writers were fond of comparing the *pampas* with the ocean. And they were right, Verity thought, as she watched the landscape shimmer in the growing heat of the day. It was like a strange motionless surface, gently stirred by the breeze that blew continually over it. The general effect was hypnotic. She could feel her eyes closing and jerked herself upright in an effort to stay awake. She was not going to fall asleep, she told herself.

He noticed, of course. He never seemed to miss a thing where she was concerned. 'It's another two hours to Córdoba. Why not take a nap?' He threw her a wicked look. 'Use my shoulder as a pillow, if you like. It won't be the first time.'

She did not suppose it would be; she was not that naïve. 'No, thank you, I'm fine as I am.' Did he really think she would adopt the casual intimacy that he shared with his women friends? He had another think coming, if he did! Verity leaned her head against the metal of the window frame and dozed uncomfortably.

She came round with a start as the car swerved suddenly. 'What's the matter?' she asked.

'A cow on the road. Move, you stupid animal,' he said without heat, as the cow raced frantically along the road in front of them, apparently incapable of turning off into the safety of the open ground on either side of the road. He slowed to a crawl, then, as the animal finally came to its senses and pounded off the road, speeded on again.

'They're like that. They don't think things out,' said Verity.

'Typically female,' he commented. 'One idea in mind and hellbent on clinging to it.'

He had not taken his glance off the road. He was not even speaking to her directly, but to a point somewhere on the far horizon. Verity took his drift, though. 'You think I'm like that, do you?'

'If the cap fits,' he said carelessly.

'Meaning I should reconsider my opinion of you?' she asked.

'Blind prejudice usually springs from ignorance or stupidity,' he told her calmly. 'And you're neither ignorant nor stupid.'

'Thanks for the compliment! From a razor-sharp mind like yours it's quite a concession.'

'You're determined not to like me, aren't you?' he accused.

'Does it matter so much to you?'

'Not at all,' he said. 'We'll play it your way, if that's what you want. The end result will be the same.'

What did he mean by that? Verity felt suddenly uneasy. He had capitulated just now, hadn't he? He had told her it no longer mattered to him what she thought of him. In the future she could go her own road without let or hindrance from him. That was what he had been saying, wasn't it?

But Ramón Vance did not give up that easily, she was sure. It was a trap of some kind, she was certain of it. She glanced warily across at him and he caught her before she had time to look away.

'Worried?' he asked her.

'No, why should I be?'

'I don't make a fair opponent, Verity. I play dirty when it suits me.'

All's fair in love and war—the tag flashed through her mind. But Ramón Vance was not in love with her, so that was all right. 'I can imagine,' she said tartly.

'Well, don't say you didn't ask for it. And don't expect any sympathy if you get hurt in the process.'

'I shan't get hurt,' she said defiantly, and spoke to herself as much as to him.

'It would be a pity,' he told her lightly. He did not believe she could look after herself. Well, he would see!

They were on National Route Nine leading directly to Córdoba, and it was not long before the towers of the city came into view. It was a strange mix of old and new, but Verity had always loved the way that the colonial buildings nestled cheek by jowl with the office blocks and industrial plants of later times.

They followed the signs to the city centre, slowing down as they encountered more traffic on the road. Ramón was a good driver, she would allow him that, she decided. After the aggressive displays of most Argentinian men, who, once behind a wheel, drove as if they were on a racing circuit, her companion's quiet control was a great relief. But, no doubt, he felt no need to prove himself in that area. Ramón Vance would take other opportunities to demonstrate his manhood.

He parked the car not far from the Plaza San Martín in the old part of town and then turned to collect the bulky briefcase that he had left in the back seat. Suddenly he was a city businessman again; cool, hard-headed, aloof.

'I have business at the bank that will keep me there for the rest of the morning. Can you amuse yourself on your own? I expect they could find somewhere for you to sit and wait for me at the bank.'

'No, thank you.' She did not sit around and wait for any man, let alone Ramón Vance. 'I was at school near here for ten years—I think I just about know my way about.'

Sarcasm was wasted on him. 'Fine. Do you know the Crillon?'

'Yes, of course. But——'

'I'll see you there at two o'clock for lunch. Try not to be late.'

He gave her a brief nod of dismissal, as if she had been a servant, she thought indignantly, and vanished down the narrow street that led towards the main commercial area of the city. How typical of the man not even to ask her if she wanted to join him for lunch! He just assumed that she would fall in with whatever plans he made. High-handed, arrogant, domineering swine that he was! She wondered what he would do if she did not turn up and smiled at the idea. Had anyone ever stood him up? she wondered. It would be a not-able first for him.

But just because Ramón Vance was an unreasonable character there was no excuse for her to emulate him and be equally bad-mannered, she decided as two o'clock approached and hunger pangs assailed her. She could, of course, make her way to any one of the little cafés around the pedestrian centre where she had just spent a happy few hours browsing in the little boutiques that abounded there, but the Crillon was one of the best eating places in Córdoba and it seemed a pity to pass up the chance of an excellent meal there just because her lunch escort was not to her liking. She headed for Rivadavia, passing the lovely baroque cathedral as she went.

Ramón was waiting for her in the reception area of the hotel. The morning had clearly gone well for him: he looked relaxed and there was a decided air of accomplishment about him. He appeared not to notice the admiring looks that he was attracting from the Crillon's female clientele, but Verity was acutely conscious of the scrutiny she received when she joined him. *Probably wondering what a dowdy-looking girl like me is doing in his company,* she thought. But *she* did not care what they thought. Her head lifted defiantly in response.

'We'll go straight in, if you're ready,' said Ramón, as he greeted her. 'It's good to find a woman who arrives on time. I expected you to be at least another ten minutes.'

'Punctuality is one of my few virtues,' she said sweetly, letting him guide her towards the dining-room. She had no intention of telling him how close he was to not seeing her at all. If she had carried out her original plan of eating on her own, he would still have been pacing the floor in an hour's time or more.

'And no bags or parcels either. Another virtue, or did you leave them in the cloakroom?'

'No money,' she explained simply. 'But I enjoyed myself window-shopping.'

He frowned. 'You should have told me. I would have lent you some cash. I had plenty with me.'

'Why should you?' she asked coolly. 'I'm not your responsibility.'

He gave her a speaking glance, but did not pursue the subject. His good mood of the moment evidently precluded arguments. Either that or his reluctance to have a stand-up row with her in the middle of one of Córdoba's plushest hotels. Although she could not imagine him worrying too much about appearances. He followed his own rules, not those laid down by other people.

He saw her seated and took his own chair across the table from her. They had one of the best positions in the restaurant, discreetly hidden from view, but able to see the rest of the room. A perfect place for a rend-ezvous. Verity wondered if the waiter thought they were lovers to put them in this setting. A handsome couple, they said of engaged people. She smiled. No one could say that of her and Ramón Vance; a more disparate pair could hardly be imagined.

Menus appeared before them as if by magic and she studied the selection of food in silence. Her father had brought her here once for afternoon tea as a great treat and special occasion. 'A meal here would just about break the bank,' he had joked, 'so make the most of those cream cakes!' As she looked at the wide selection of dishes available Verity was hardly surprised. This was gracious living and no mistake!

'What will you have?' Ramón Vance had made his choice and looked across at her in query.

'The fish, I think. We don't often get fresh trout at home.' Dazzled by the list, she made a quick decision.

'Good.' Whether he was approving her choice or merely the speed with which she made up her mind, she did not know. 'I'll join the lady.' He gave the order to a hovering, attentive waiter and chose a wine to

accompany the meal without consulting Verity. Not
that it worried her. She knew remarkably little about
the subject and cared still less, although she enjoyed
the Argentinian wines that her father liked to sample
on high days and holidays.

The details disposed of satisfactorily, Ramón Vance
sat back in his chair, entirely at his ease as he glanced
round the room with a faintly critical eye.

'Well, does it meet with your high standards?' She
could not resist putting the question.

'It'll do,' he said casually. 'It makes a change, at any
rate.'

'I suppose you lunch at much grander places in
Buenos Aires.'

He looked amused. 'Hardly. Usually a sandwich in
the office if I'm lucky, and often I don't get that when
I'm busy. If I want to linger over a meal I wait until
the evening.'

With soft lights, sweet music and the woman of his
choice, Verity supposed. For a brief moment she let
her imagination rove and wondered what it would be
like to dine with him as his favoured lady of the
moment. He probably changed his women nearly as
often as his shirts, she thought, but while he was dancing attendance he would act as if one was the only
woman in the world. He would charm and flatter and
say all the things that one wanted to hear. And one
would be a little bit in love with him, but not too much,
because that was the way to get hurt.

'I've never been to Buenos Aires,' she told him wist-
fully. 'Years ago, when I was about eight or nine years
old, Dad went to the Palermo Agricultural Show one
July. He was going to take me with him. He promised
me he'd show me all the sights in town—the Plaza de
Mayo, the President's palace, that little Italian quarter

near the port——'

'La Boca, they call it,' he told her. 'I know it well. But something stopped you from going?'

'Measles,' she said ruefully. 'I cried for two days solid, I think. I was so miserable! All my life I'd been hearing about Buenos Aires. It was like a fairy tale city to me—and to have the chance of seeing it at last suddenly snatched away from me was too much to bear!'

He laughed, genuinely amused by her story. 'There'll be other times. You're young yet. And when you do get there, you'll be much more able to appreciate what it has to offer than when you were eight years old. Think of the exclusive shops in the Calle Florida. They're enough to gladden any female heart. They rival Paris for sophistication. There's the theatre, the opera at the Teatro Colón, the museums and art galleries. And, when you're sick of culture, you can join the fashionable crowds at the race track or watch polo players at Palermo.'

'It sounds wonderful. You must enjoy living there.'

He shrugged. 'At first. I was a country boy and it dazzled me. Later still I found the ceaseless round of socialising rather a bore.'

Verity tried to imagine him fresh from the country, naïve and easily conned. It was an impossible picture. Ramón Vance had been born to dominate whichever environment he chose to live in. Not for him the agonies of indecision or selfconsciousness! The jaded sophisticate of today must have been recognisable even in his earlier years.

'Dad told me that you came from an *estancia* near Rosario,' she commented.

He paused while the waiter brought the wine of his choice for him to sample and then nodded his approval of it. Verity could not help noticing that instead of a local vineyard the name on the bottle was a French one. He must have money to splash around, she thought. She had heard her father mention the prohibitive cost of imported wines these days. He dined in style, did Ramón Vance.

'Yes,' he said finally, in answer to her. 'It wasn't so very different from Vista Hermosa. A little smaller, perhaps. And our home lacked the decaying grandeur of yours.'

Verity glanced quickly at him, registering a slight to her housekeeping abilities, then decided to let it pass. 'Were you a large family?' she asked him. She was suddenly curious to find out more about the man, eager to discover what had made him the way he was today.

'Myself and my brother. Our mother died when we were still both at school. My brother left to help on the ranch. I stayed on to get my *bachillerato*, the qualification I needed for university. But I helped out in the holidays and later, in between studies.'

Hence his uncanny skill with the stockwhip and his complete understanding of all matters agricultural. No wonder the men at Vista Hermosa spoke so highly of his knowledge and solutions to their problems!

'And then?' She paused, taking a sip of her wine. It was cold and refreshing and it slid down her throat like nectar.

'My father died. If we'd split our inheritance as he intended, it would have meant a struggle for each of us to survive. So I let my brother have the ranch and went to the city to make my own way in the world.'

'That was good of you,' she said impulsively.

He searched her face as if expecting to find sarcasm there and seeing none gave a faint smile. 'Yes, it was, wasn't it? And virtue brought its own rewards. My brother still struggles to make ends meet, while I have everything that money can buy.'

'Happiness?' Verity asked.

'As much as any man can expect, all things considered,' he said carelessly. 'I have a nice home in the best part of town. I drive a Lancia. I have the money in the bank to buy anything that I want, within reason. What more can a man ask?'

'A lot more.' Verity waited until she had been served with the dish of her choice and then returned to the argument. 'There are things that money can't buy.'

'Are there?' he asked cynically. 'I wouldn't have thought so.'

'What about friends? I don't mean hangers on, but people who care about you and what happens to you. People that you can go to when you need help.'

The arrogant features mocked her. 'I'm remarkably self-sufficient in that respect,' he told her. 'I tend not to need any assistance in running my life.'

She tried another tack. 'All right. What about family life? Money can't buy you a wife and children.'

He laughed harshly. 'I'm sure it could, if I wanted them. I think there'd be quite a lot of applicants if I advertised the post.'

He would not need to advertise the fact that he was in the market for a wife, she acknowledged. She had no doubt that, in the past, any number of women had tried to get his ring on their fingers. Without a penny to his name Ramón Vance would draw women to him. His was that kind of attraction. He would only have to lift a hand and he would get the attention he wanted. And he knew it.

She went on with her meal in silence, aware that he was studying her across the table. Was he wondering why the magic did not seem to work in her case?

'You're very cynical,' she accused.

'I'd prefer to call myself realistic. I like a simple life without too many complications. If they threaten, I cut loose. It's as simple as that.'

'By complications, you mean women, I suppose?' Verity asked. She had never talked like this to a man before and she was finding it a strangely stimulating experience. Discussing life and love with her schoolgirl confidantes, as lacking in worldly knowledge as herself, was not the same as talking to Ramón Vance. What he did not know about life in the big world probably wasn't worth knowing. 'And how many hearts have you broken in the process?'

'Hardly any,' he said indifferently. 'Your sex is a good deal tougher than it pretends.'

Perhaps he was right. No doubt the women with whom he came into contact were eminently capable of looking after themselves. They did not need a warning. They knew the score. They did not look for protestations of love or promises of marriage before they surrendered to a man. They probably found brief liaisons satisfying. Verity could not imagine herself reacting that way; it was not in her nature. Yet Ramón Vance had awakened a lot of emotions that she had not thought she possessed.

She toyed with her food, pushing it round her plate. She had no appetite all of a sudden. She waited for him to finish. She was being silly, she told herself, to let the man get to her in this way. Did it really matter what he thought? He was a ship in the night, pausing for a while and then passing on. In six months' time she would have forgotten him. She raised her eyes and met his faintly searching look.

'Have I disillusioned you?' he asked.

'No.' That, at least, was true. Even before she had

met him she had had a fair idea of how ruthless he could be. 'I stopped believing in story-book heroes a long time ago.'

'Just as well,' he said casually. 'They're a bit thin on the ground these days.'

'Yes,' she agreed. She turned her attention to the sweets trolley that was being wheeled alongside for her inspection and pretended an interest she was far from feeling in the selection before her as if the subject they had been discussing no longer mattered.

They talked of other things after that—safe, non-controversial topics such as the weather, music, art and sport. Ramón knew something about almost everything, Verity discovered, and when he chose to exert himself, he could be fascinating. She was genuinely surprised when she glanced at her watch to find that over two hours had passed with a degree of pleasure that she would never have imagined possible earlier in the day. She wondered if that fact had struck him as well.

It had. As he strode beside her as they left the restaurant his hand brushed against her arm and she flinched at the contact. She did not know why. She was not usually so jumpy with people. But Ramón Vance wasn't just people. He had a greater impact, somehow.

'Is the truce over, then?' he asked, registering the gesture.

'Was there one?'

'I thought that in there,' he jerked a dark head in the direction from which they had just come, 'hostilities relaxed to a certain extent.'

'Well, you thought wrong,' Verity lied. 'My feelings haven't changed at all.' Did he think that she was so easily won over to be charmed by pleasant manners and conversation? It was the man himself who mattered, and he had shown her his true colours.

'It's a pity,' he shrugged.

'For whom?'

'For you,' he informed her. And, without looking to see if she was following him, he strode on.

CHAPTER SIX

VERITY was surprised to see Isabel Delgado appear at Vista Hermosa the following day. She had never particularly liked the other girl and there had been little enough contact between them. Isabel had her father's habit of treating everyone in a faintly patronising manner, considering neighbours as lesser mortals to be ignored unless there was a good reason for cultivating them. Evidently her visit had a purpose; for all her polite noises it was not just a social call.

'I hear you have a house guest.' After ten minutes of carefully maintained small talk Isabel finally reached her objective.

So that was it. 'Yes.' Verity was not feeling in a communicative mood where Ramón Vance was concerned. Yesterday's trip to Córdoba had ended in a silent drive home and the prospect of future hostilities. She had had about as much as she could take of that man at the moment.

'I heard about him from my father, you understand.' Isabel was delicately concerned lest Verity should suspect her of indulging in village gossip. The Delgados did not stoop so low. 'And then yesterday, in Córdoba, I was with a friend at the Crillon, and we saw you there. That *was* Señor Vance that you were with?'

'Yes, that was him,' Verity said shortly.

If Isabel heard the brusqueness in the reply she did not heed it. 'He's a very attractive man. I had no idea he was like that.'

Like a sleek dark fox setting all the chickens in the

hen-house in a stir, thought Verity, but she did not voice the idea. 'He's all right, I suppose,' she conceded, 'if you like that kind of good looks.'

'Are you telling me you don't? You seemed to be finding him absorbing company.' Isabel's tone was faintly malicious. 'You were hanging on his every word. I tried twice to attract your attention, but you just weren't looking in any other direction but his.'

Had it really looked like that? Verity hastened to put the record straight. 'Appearances are deceptive. I can't stand the man.'

'Really? I wonder why.' The other girl's brown eyes took on a speculative expression.

'Does there have to be a reason?'

'There usually is. And he seems enough to bowl any woman off her feet. *Tiene mucho gancho.*'

Isabel had not learnt that phrase in the correct, rather formal Delgado household, Verity thought. 'Yes, he's got sex appeal, *machismo*, whatever else you like to call it. But he's also rude, overbearing and a male chauvinist of the worst type.'

Isabel seemed encouraged rather than put off by the description. She shrugged. 'One does not want a man who cannot assert himself. Strength is a good quality in a prospective husband.'

'Are you considering Ramón Vance in that light?'

'A girl must marry some time. It's inevitable unless one wishes to dwindle into spinsterhood.' Isabel's look of disdain showed what she thought of *that* prospect. 'And, if Mr Right comes along, it's best to accept the fact and snap him up.'

'Always supposing that the feeling's mutual.'

'Even if it isn't.' She gave a satisfied smile. 'A clever woman can always find ways of bringing a man round to her way of thinking. A clever, attractive woman, that is.' She glanced with faint contempt at Verity's casual appearance. Jeans and a faded cotton blouse were clearly not the marks of an attractive woman. She stroked her own expensive-looking silk dress with a complacent air. 'One has to know how to present oneself in the best light, of course.'

'I wouldn't know about that.'

'No. You'll learn some day, I expect,' Isabel said carelessly. Verity seethed and bit back a tart retort only with a great effort. 'After all, I am two years older than you are.'

But not much wiser, if she thought that she was going to ensnare Ramón Vance just by setting her sights at him. He must have had more matrimonial snares laid out for him than the average man and he had dodged them all up till now. Was it likely that he would fall prey to Isabel Delgado? Verity doubted it somehow. Not that there was any point in arguing further with the girl—she was too used to getting her own way to anticipate any problems of that nature. But she would find out soon enough that she had bitten off more than she could chew.

And, talking of chewing, Isabel would have to watch her consumption of sweet, sticky cakes, if she wanted to attract any man, let alone Ramón Vance. She would be as plump as her mother if she did not take care, Verity thought as she poured her guest more tea and offered a plate of biscuits to her. Pleasing curves were one thing, but a double chin and a weight problem were something else again.

Isabel lingered as long as she could. Her frequent glances through the window to the pastures outside showed that her interest lay in the prospect of Ramón's return to the house rather than in Verity's conversation. But, as time wore on, and it became clear that she

would have to leave with her curiosity about him un-
satisfied, she was forced to get to her feet and take her
leave with as good a grace as she could manage.

'How stupid of me! I nearly forgot my mother's invitation—and that was the only reason that I came.'
She gave a false laugh that did not deceive Verity for a
moment.

Not quite the only reason, Verity thought, but did
not say so. 'An invitation?' she queried. 'How very nice
of your mother. It must be nearly a year since we were
last over at Los Molinos.' And even then it had been
as fill-ins to make up the numbers round Señora
Delgado's vast, antique dining table when someone
else had been taken ill. Good manners forbade her
mentioning that, but her tone conveyed a pointed reminder of the fact.

'Is it really that long? Surely not.' Isabel contrived
to sound surprised. 'Doesn't time fly? I'd never have
thought it. All the more reason for you to come over as
soon as possible. What about Thursday evening? Just
a simple family meal, you understand. Nothing elabor-
ate, of course.' Her glance rested again on Verity's
clothes as if to underline the point that there was no
need to dress up. 'I suppose you'll be free?' Her tone
said, you usually are.

Verity suppressed a sigh. She would have liked
nothing better than to reject the invitation with every
appearance of distaste. Let Isabel have a refusal for
once! What a pity that she had been brought up good-
mannered. Instead she had to smile and say thank you
with apparent sincerity.

'Yes, I think that we're free that evening,' she said,
trying to sound enthusiastic. 'I'll have to check with
Dad, of course, but we should be able to manage it.
Please thank your mother for inviting us both.'

Although goodness knew why she had bothered. Unless Señor Delgado felt that he owed a meal in return for the dinner that he had had with her father and Ramón Vance a short time ago. He was a fairly punctilious man about returning favours.

'The three of you, actually,' Isabel corrected her.

'You mean——'

The other girl gave her a faint, pitying smile that explained all. 'Señor Vance will be coming with you, naturally. He will be a very welcome guest.'

Unlike Verity and her father, who were only there because Ramón Vance happened to be staying with them. 'I see,' said Verity. 'Well, I'll certainly pass on the invitation. But I can't say whether he'll be able to accept.'

'Oh, I think you'll find that he will. Poor man! After Buenos Aires he must be finding life in the sticks abominably dull. He must be pining for some decent entertainment among civilised people.'

'As if we were peasants or something!' Verity told her father indignantly when she passed on the news of the invitation to him later that day. 'And I suppose she thinks that they're the cream of society. She makes me sick, that girl. I suppose she can't help it. She must get her manners from her parents. No one could actually be born that rude!'

Mark Williams laughed. 'You must have had quite an afternoon putting up with her.'

'I did. I don't know how I kept my hands off her.'

'We'll have to go, of course. They'd take offence if we didn't. But they'll probably be so busy lionising our guest that they won't have time to waste on making us feel out of place and underlining the difference between us.'

'Pack of snobs,' commented Verity inelegantly.

'What's Isabel doing with herself these days?'

She shrugged. 'Waiting for a husband to come along. She thinks Ramón Vance might fit the bill nicely.' She smiled at the thought. 'What with Señora Delgado sounding out his prospects and Isabel throwing out inviting glances he should be in for quite an evening, if he deigns to honour them with his presence.'

'No reason why he shouldn't. I'll ask him.'

The necessary consent obtained, Verity rang Los Molinos with the news. Señora Delgado was at her most gracious and when she had rung off Verity permitted herself a smile of amusement. It was amazing how differently people reacted to Ramón Vance. At Vista Hermosa he was an unwelcome visitor—at least as far as Verity was concerned. But at Los Molinos he was an honoured guest to be wooed and flattered as a prospective catch for Isabel. Well, she was welcome to him if she succeeded.

Verity hoped the Delgados would not make too much fuss over the arrangements, but she had a horrid suspicion that they would. She reviewed her wardrobe gloomily, knowing that she had nothing to compare with Isabel's expensive gowns. A simple evening with the family, that was how Isabel had described it, but Verity had no doubt that the women of the Delgado household would be dressed up to the nines.

On Thursday evening she stood in front of her mirror and regarded her reflection with something like despair. She had only one outfit that was remotely suitable for the occasion: a long, severely cut black skirt that teamed with a white blouse, vividly decorated with embroidered flowers in all colours of the rainbow. Verity had always felt confident that she looked good in the ensemble, but now she had doubts.

She looked what she was—a schoolgirl. There was

nothing remotely sophisticated about her. She frowned. As an experiment she dragged back her hair, fastening it in a slide, but chestnut tendrils escaped from it even as she stood back to look at the result and she wrenched it off again with an impatient hand, cursing as she did so. Even her make-up was simple. She did not know how to make dramatic eyes with the skilful application of shadow and mascara. And now was clearly not the time to experiment. Ramón Vance would only laugh at her if she turned up looking like a clown, because the effect had gone wrong.

She took a final dissatisfied look at herself, then picked up her shawl and went to join her escorts for the evening. It was all right if you were a man, she thought a little bitterly. You wore your best suit and a clean shirt and tie. No need to worry what the other men would be wearing, and if someone was spotted in the identical outfit it was a matter for self-congratulation, not horror. Men did not have to think about colour combinations or shades of make-up or care if their noses were shiny. And women went through all those agonies just for male gratification. It was so unfair!

The two men were standing in the entrance hall, and Verity apologised swiftly for keeping them waiting.

'It was worth it, love.' Her father had no complaints to make—she could tell from the look of pride on his face as he studied her appearance. 'You're charming this evening. Isn't she, Vance?' He turned to the silent man by his side for confirmation.

The dark eyes swept her from head to foot with a slow deliberation that made her feel acutely selfconscious—as he no doubt intended. Did he have to look at her as if she was a prime piece of beef on the hoof?

'Very attractive,' he said gravely at last, and she could have hit him for taking so long.

'Shall we go?' she asked hastily. 'It's a tricky drive in the dark and we don't want to be late.'

'Señora Delgado would have our blood,' Mark Williams agreed, and led the way to the car.

It had been decided that Ramón would drive them to Los Molinos, his Land Rover being more respectable than the battered jalopy that was used for work about the *estancia*. 'We can't turn up smelling of cattle disinfectant,' her father had said jokingly, and Verity had concurred. Now she moved ahead of her father, intending to sit in the back seat, but he forestalled her.

'Spread yourself out in the front seat,' he told her firmly. 'You'll only crush your dress getting into the back.'

There was no point making a fuss, although she was sorely tempted to argue the question. Ramón Vance was standing there, holding the door and waiting for her to get in. She submitted meekly, hunching herself up at one end of the long front seat, keeping as much distance as possible between herself and the driver.

Ramón gave no sign of noticing her strategy as he took that seat, but, as the car lurched off the main road and on to the twisting track that was the shortest route to Los Molinos, she saw a look of amusement cross his features as he registered the difficulty she was having in maintaining her position as the movement of the vehicle became jerkier and less easy to predict.

'Still keeping me at arm's length?' he mocked her softly after one pothole in the road, which would have jerked her nearly on to his lap if she had not clutched the window-frame like grim death. 'You'll give in eventually, you know.'

'Not if I can help it,' she said fiercely, then glanced

anxiously behind her, wondering if the noise of the engine had masked her words from her father. He liked Ramón Vance and she tried hard to spare him the knowledge that, for once, they did not agree.

It was a relief to see the lights of Los Molinos coming into view. They were honoured indeed, she noticed, for the Delgados, hearing the sound of the car approaching, had come to the door of the house to greet their guests, instead of following their usual practice of leaving the duty to the resident housekeeper.

Introductions were made and they were shepherded inside to the *salón*, a long, gracious room, exquisitely decorated and furnished with tasteful antiques. A little different from its counterpart at Vista Hermosa, Verity acknowledged ruefully, and, catching the guest of honour's eye, could tell that he was making the same judgment. Her chin tilted in defiant response and she saw him smile at the gesture. Damn the man! Did he have to be a mind-reader?

'You'll take some sherry before dinner.' It was a statement rather than an invitation, and Señor Delgado waved to a smartly-dressed servant, indicating that she should serve the tray of drinks that she was holding in readiness. That was the trouble with the Delgado family, Verity thought as she accepted her drink and sipped it meekly. They liked to take control and it never occurred to them that other people might have different ideas. She wondered what Ramón Vance would make of that approach. It was one he used himself with total success. Would he resent it in others?

If he did, he certainly gave no sign of the fact. His dark features were urbane as he allowed Señora Delgado to monopolise him for a few minutes before a quick, imperative jerk of her head summoned Isabel to their side to join the conversation. Verity saw the look of appreciation she received from Ramón, very different from the complacent glance that her mother gave her. It was the way a man looked at a woman in whom he was interested; a lingering, admiring gaze that caressed as it roved over her figure and rested slightly longer on the glowing face that was turned eagerly up to his.

Verity had to admit that the other girl was looking good tonight. Of course it helped to be able to patronise any shop in Córdoba without having to think too much about the price one was paying, and having a maid who could dress one's hair to perfection was a distinct advantage. The scarlet dress that Isabel wore outlined every curve of a distinctly unboyish figure, clinging in all the right places where a man was concerned. Perhaps it was cut slightly on the low side, showing off rather more of Isabel's ample bosom than good taste would have suggested, but Ramón was not offended. On the contrary, he was smiling down at her in a most suggestively intent way.

Verity turned away and, listening to her father's conversation with Señor Delgado, tried to distance herself from what was happening across the room. But last year's alfalfa figures were not of absorbing interest to her, however hard she kept her mind on them, and she found her glance straying more than once to the other side of the room.

Isabel had drawn her guest to a small sofa and was patting the seat by her side in an inviting manner that seemed to be entertaining him greatly. Of Señora Delgado there was no sign. Presumably she had slipped away to make sure that the final touches were being correctly added to the meal. Neither of them seemed to be missing her, Verity thought, as she studied the two dark heads bent close, sharing some joke together.

It meant nothing to him, of course. It was just a highly skilled technique that years of practice had polished to perfection. He did not really care about Isabel. Or did he? One never knew with a man like that, Verity told herself bitterly. He could don any number of masks and, unless he chose, no woman would be able to dig below the surface to the real man and his thoughts underneath. She gave herself a mental shake. What was there for her to brood about? Let Isabel try her luck and welcome. She should be glad it wasn't herself. She *was* glad, Verity told herself.

And then, suddenly, he looked up and caught and held her gaze in a quizzical, slightly mocking hold. Verity wanted to turn away, but somehow she wasn't able to, that mesmerising glance pinning her like a butterfly, a reluctant captive.

She amused him, she could tell, as a dark brow quirked in pure devilment at her, registering her isolation before returning his interest to whatever Isabel was saying to him. A gentleman would have come over and rescued her and included her in a conversation more to her taste than farming facts and worries. But Ramón Vance was no gentleman—he had told her as much himself. As far as he was concerned she could stew for the rest of the evening while he amused himself in his own way.

He continued to do so at the dinner table, when they moved from the *salón* into the equally splendid dining room. Seated between Isabel and her mother in the position of honour, he was an attentive guest, dividing his time between his hostess and her daughter, with Isabel receiving the lion's share of his notice. It was just as well that the girl had the field to herself, thought Verity bitchily. In her best outfit she was no rival to Isabel, and she acknowledged it. But either of Isabel's sisters might have given her a run for her money. They were both more attractive than she was. Verity supposed they had been sent to bed early. At sixteen and eighteen respectively they were still young enough to find dinner parties a bore—although Verity was willing to bet that they would have found something to interest them at this one.

'And how is life with you now that you are a lady of leisure?' Señor Delgado was asking with the heavy gallantry that he always affected with the female sex. 'Time must lie very heavily on your hands now that you are no longer at school.'

What different worlds they inhabited! The Delgado girls would know nothing of her life, struggling to keep the rambling, enormous *estancia* house in some kind of order, as well as cooking and cleaning for her father and now for their uninvited guest. At Los Molinos there were servants to deal with that sort of thing. What boring lives Isabel and her sisters must lead! Not that she could say so. It might sound like sour grapes.

'Oh, I manage to find quite a lot to keep me busy.' With an effort she turned her attention from the other side of the table where Isabel was devoting herself wholeheartedly to Ramón. 'I run the house, you know.'

'Yes. What will your father do when you marry and leave him?'

'I shouldn't think that will be for a long time yet.' If ever, she added silently. Marriage seemed an impossible prospect at the moment. She had nothing to recommend her to a man. Not looks, not money, not anything.

Señor Delgado wagged a roguish finger at her. 'He'll be along before you know it, will Mr Right. It happens to every girl sooner or later. My own Imelda was only seventeen when we were married, but Isabel here is over twenty and still single. And her sisters catching her up fast.' His eyes strayed to his daughter, who was listening, wide-eyed, to some anecdote that Ramón Vance was telling. Verity caught a look of faint satisfaction on his face. Señora Delgado was not the only matchmaker in the family, although she was more obvious about it than her husband. Ramón Vance would do very well as a prospective son-in-law.

Verity did not enjoy the meal, although the food and drink were superb. At any other time the seafood cocktail, followed by steak garnished with ham and pâté de foie gras, would have delighted her. Tonight it could have been completely tasteless for all the pleasure that she derived from it. She drank slightly more than usual, although the heavy red wine was not really to her liking. The evening seemed interminable. She tried to look surreptitiously at her watch, but Ramón saw her and she started guiltily, knocking over her wine glass in the process.

'Oh, I'm sorry!' Verity watched the red stain spread over the immaculate linen and dabbed ineffectually at it with her napkin.

'It doesn't matter. The servants will deal with it later.' But Señora Delgado's voice held a note of frosty disapproval. Clearly it would be the last time that peasants who did not know their table manners were invited to Los Molinos. Verity drank her coffee in silence, hardly daring to draw attention to her presence at the table, although she was grateful for her father's whispered words of encouragement, before he engaged Señora Delgado in a long discussion that was calculated to take her mind off Verity's shortcomings.

It was after midnight before the Delgados let them go. Or rather before they were willing to part with

Ramón Vance, Verity thought sourly as they bumped their way back along the track to Vista Hermosa. As far as she and her father were concerned they could have left hours ago with the Delgados' blessing. It was their guest who had made a big hit.

'We will see you again soon?' Isabel had asked anxiously, her small, beautifully manicured hand resting against the dark sleeve of his jacket as the Vista Hermosa party had made their farewells.

If ever a girl was throwing herself at a man, this was it. Verity watched the scene scornfully. *She* would never wear her heart on her sleeve quite so openly for any man—let alone a wolf like Ramón Vance!

'I'll be in touch,' he told her carelessly, and Verity saw the other girl's face signify her pleasure. Trusting little fool! Or was she just so keen to get a husband that she did not care what an exhibition she made of herself? That was probably it. Idly Verity wondered how much pressure was being put on Isabel to find a husband. She certainly did not look as if it was an effort for her to be very pleasant to the guest of honour tonight. But perhaps she was as eager to escape from the rather restricting Delgado household as her parents were for her to leave it as the wife of some successful man. Perhaps Ramón Vance fitted the bill for everyone. And they were welcome to him as far as she was concerned.

Verity studied him as they drove. Her father had nodded off in the back of the car and the sound of his snores punctuated the silence, making conversation unnecessary. She was glad of that, she thought, half awake, half asleep herself, although the man in the driving seat seemed as fresh as he had been on the earlier journey. The darkness was kind to him. It concealed the arrogance in his face, obscured the firmness of his chin and blurred the strong line of his nose. In the faint light he looked more human, more approachable. Approachable—that was a joke! She would rather cuddle up to a piranha fish. At least you knew where you were with them. She heard someone laugh aloud and realised that it was her. Goodness, she must have had more to drink than she thought!

His mind was running on the same lines. 'Something amusing you?' he asked lazily. 'Or is it just too much good red wine? I noticed that you were enjoying it, if that's the word.'

'I'm surprised you noticed anything,' she accused him. 'You were far too busy gazing into Isabel's eyes to spare any time for me.'

'Does that rankle? I thought it might.'

'I couldn't care less,' she said loftily, but spoiled the effect with a yawn. She did not feel like arguing; she wanted to go to sleep.

The fresh air hit her like a mule's kick when they reached Vista Hermosa, and she staggered as she walked towards the house.

'Are you still claiming that you're as sober as a judge?' That hateful voice sounded in her ear and a strong arm came round her, supporting her. 'Lean against me,' he commanded her.

'I'm fine.' She wanted to push him away, declare her independence, but somehow she could not find the strength and instead leaned thankfully against him as he steered her towards the house.

'Is she all right?' Verity heard her father's voice in the background as they entered the front door and she blinked as the lights were switched on.

'Just tired, and slightly the worse for Delgado's red wine.' The younger man's voice was briskly impersonal. 'Go to bed, Williams. You look all in your-

self. I'll deal with her. She needs a hot drink or she'll
have one heck of a head when she wakes up in the
morning.'

'If you're sure?' Verity heard her father's mutter of
assent, and then his called 'goodnight' as he disappeared down the corridor in the direction of his own
room. A hot drink was probably a good idea, although
she did not need Ramón Vance's help to get it. She
allowed him to guide her in the direction of the kitchen,
but protested as he dumped her neatly in a chair and
left her to look for what he needed to make the drink.

'Coffee all right?' he asked, getting it out of the cupboard. 'It's what you need right now and I don't suppose it'll keep you awake. I doubt if a tank regiment
rolling through your bedroom could do that tonight.'

'I'll get it myself. I'm not incapable, you know.' She
got cautiously to her feet and was glad to find that the
room had stopped swirling round her. She was not
drunk. Just a little giddy, perhaps. She was not used
to that much rich food and wine.

'You could have fooled me a moment ago.' Ramón
ignored her outstretched hand and continued to spoon
instant coffee into the mugs that he had found, then
filled the kettle and set it to boil on the old-fashioned
range. 'Or was that just a ploy?'

'To get your arms around me?' She did not pretend
to misunderstand him. 'Hardly. *I'm* not that desperate.'

'And Isabel is? Is that what you mean?'

'Well, she certainly wasn't a blushing violet tonight, was she? She did all she could to keep your attention.'

'I was her guest,' he pointed out calmly. 'Did you
expect her to ignore me? Anyway, why the inquisition?
You sound like a nagging wife!'

'What would you know about marriage? You've never tried it.'

'Enough to keep well clear,' he said. He retrieved the kettle and poured the steaming water into the mugs, pushing one of them towards her. 'Here, have your coffee and stop making such a fuss.'

'I'm not making a fuss!' she hissed indignantly at him.

'It sounds like it to me. I thought you couldn't care less about my feelings for Isabel.'

'Her or any other girl. It's just that I find it disgusting to watch someone throwing herself at your head quite as obviously as she did tonight.'

'Liar,' he said without heat. 'I saw you looking at us and it wasn't disgust in your eyes. It was envy.'

'You're deluding yourself,' she told him contemptuously, even as she wondered if he might be right. Had she envied Isabel? Had she wanted him to pay her the same flattering degree of attention that he had shown to the other girl? Surely not.

'I don't think so. I know women. And you're all woman, Verity, even if you don't have any idea of your full potential as yet. You wanted me with you. If you're honest, you'll admit that you still do.'

Verity was not going to admit anything of the kind. She stared at the rapidly cooling coffee that sat untouched on the table at her side and tried to think of an adequate reply. He caught one off balance, did Ramón Vance, and she lacked his speed of recovery.

He took a step towards her and then another, and she stood there as if rooted to the spot. She should move, she told herself, but a stronger voice was telling her to stay exactly where she was, and she listened to it.

'Lost for words?' he mocked her. 'That's not like you, Verity.'

It wasn't. Her mouth felt suddenly dry. The silence between them was deafening and she could feel a pounding in her ears. His arms went round her and she made no attempt to push him away. Unresisting, she let him pull her towards him, moulding her to the hard strength of his body.

'Don't you want this?' he asked her softly as his lips traced a fiery path along the side of her neck, travelling upwards to brush her quivering mouth. 'Don't you want this?' One hand moved to caress her breast, arousing strange, feverish sensations that coursed through her, leaving her trembling and pliant to his touch. It was more than any woman could stand, this skilled lovemaking.

Her lips opened to say she didn't know what, and then she was lost. His mouth had covered hers with a hard demand, and response leapt in her. She pressed herself against him, glorying in the feel of him against her as he took her into realms that she had never known existed. All her senses were alive in a blaze of pleasure. Her hands reached up to unbutton his shirt and to spread themselves against the hair-roughened skin of his chest, and she made no protest as her own blouse opened to his seeking hands and she felt him stroke her breasts to throbbing life.

She wanted him—she admitted it now with every move of her body, every incoherent murmur of his name. 'Ramón, Ramón!' It was the first time that she had called him that, but the words left her lips quite naturally. He was no longer the man she hated, the man who had brought her so much disruption, the man who held their future in the balance. He was someone who had awakened her to a fever-pitch of undiscovered emotions, and she loved him for it.

But sanity came flooding back when she felt him

pushing her towards the door. Where was he taking her? What was he doing? From somewhere she found the strength to resist him and push her hands against his chest in a gesture that stayed him.

'What's the matter?' He sounded impatient. Looking at the flame in his eyes, she had no doubt that he was as aroused as she. He wanted her—and he wanted her now. She struggled in earnest. Suddenly she wasn't sure any more.

'I want to go to bed,' she told him.

'Wasn't that where we were heading?' He tried to pull her with him.

'On my own,' she said in a whisper. She was scared of him now.

With an effort he released her. 'You certainly pick your moments, don't you?' He stood back, breathing quickly, as stirred as she was. 'There's a word for girls like you,' he said pleasantly. 'I wonder if you've ever heard it.'

'I'm sorry.'

'Are you?' he asked harshly. 'Or did you set it up on purpose, just to try and show me what weapons you could use when you chose?'

'I'm sorry,' Verity repeated helplessly. It was a situation that she had never met before.

'You'll be even sorrier one of these fine days!' He flung the words at her as if he loathed her. 'Now get out of my sight before I do you an injury!'

And, shaking like a leaf, she fled from him.

CHAPTER SEVEN

VERITY did not want to face him next morning. After she had fled from him to the sanctuary of her room, she had undressed and washed mechanically before getting into bed. Then she had lain, tossing and turning for what seemed like hours until she had eventually fallen into a disturbed, restless sleep. She woke unrefreshed at first light, her head dull and heavy. It was an effort even to get out of bed. Was it an overdose of wine or of Ramón Vance that she was suffering from? She suspected the latter.

She wondered if she would have felt better if she had let matters take their natural course last night. Ramón had accused her of being a tease, a girl who led men on quite deliberately without any intention of offering them final fulfilment. But it had not been like that. Presumably he had experienced that mind-stretching feeling of ecstasy many times before. For her it had been a first, and she had wanted nothing more than for it to go on and lead her to the ultimate pleasure.

Yet she had called a halt. And half of her was glad that she had done so. Where was the joy in being just another name on Ramón Vance's list of conquests? That was the way to get hurt. He was the sort to take what he wanted and pass on carelessly. He did not want responsibility of the type that a wife and family brought. He was fancy free and intended to stay that way. And so did she, thought Verity with determination.

It was hard to meet his cool gaze over the breakfast table and act as if nothing had happened between them, but somehow she managed it, and knew that she had surprised him. She even managed a smile in response to her father's teasing about hardened drinkers, although it was an effort. Things would get better, she told herself. But the only real solution would be for Ramón Vance to remove himself completely from her sphere. And surely it wouldn't be long now before his business at Vista Hermosa was concluded and matters were decided one way or another?

She studied him surreptitiously across the table. A cup of strong black coffee was all that she could manage this morning, but Ramón was eating steak topped with eggs with all his usual appetite. She wished it would choke him.

Mark Williams finished his meal and got to his feet. 'I'll see you outside,' he said to their visitor. 'I've a couple of things to do first.'

Would he refer to last night now that they were alone, or was the subject dead between them? Silence stretched between them and Verity was reluctant to break it. Let *him* make the first move. Then, suddenly desperate to occupy herself, she put together a stack of plates and prepared to take them to the kitchen. So they weren't on speaking terms. So what?

'Running away? You're very good at that, aren't you, Verity?' Ramón spoke at last, his voice low, but with a definite sting in it. Last night's row was not over, merely postponed until a more opportune moment. And this was it.

'Knowing when to run is a girl's best defence,' retorted Verity.

'Yes, if she's scared.'

She faced him defiantly. 'I'm not scared of you, if

that's what you're thinking.'

'No? Just of the consequences, if you dared to get involved with me,' he commented acidly.

'It wasn't a question of involvement, and you know it as well as I do. Last night you wanted cheap, casual sex, and when I wouldn't oblige, you got annoyed.'

'That's one way of putting it,' he said.

'Is there another?' she asked furiously.

'Yes. But you're not prepared to listen.'

'Try me,' she challenged him.

'I told you I'd make you want me. And I did. No, don't attempt to deny it.' He raised a hand as she gave a sound of protest. 'If what we shared was cheap and casual, it was that on both sides. I don't happen to think so, but that's just my view. Whatever it was, you were as eager for it as I was until you suddenly changed your mind and switched off. Now *that* was cheap and casual, if you like.'

'I've said I was sorry.' She flinched at the accusation in his voice. 'What more do you want?'

'Obviously more than you're prepared to give.' He gave a harsh laugh that grated on her ears. 'Next time you decide to blow hot and cold, pick a boy of limited experience, not a man who knows the score.'

'I'll pick someone with a few manners,' she retorted. 'Nobody's ever talked to me like this.'

'Then it's about time somebody did. Tell me, will this paragon of virtue ask permission before he lays a finger on you?'

'It's better that way than being taken for granted,' she flared at him.

'Is it? Tell me after you've sampled it. Most women want to be mastered, not mollycoddled.'

'Perhaps I'm the exception that proves the rule.'

'Perhaps you're just determined to be different.'

Ramón's face was dark with anger.

'You prefer conventional womanhood as represented by Isabel, I suppose?'

'She certainly has a nicer nature than you.'

'Wide-eyed, adoring and helpless. Is that what you like?'

'After your shrewishness she's a pleasant relief.'

'I'm glad you think so. You'll be keeping out of my way in future, then?' He had hurt her, but she was not going to show it.

'Yes, I expect I will. It'll be a pleasant rest for both of us.' He paused, as if about to say something else, then, thinking better of it, pushed back his chair with an irritable hand and strode out of the room.

What was it about the man that made her lose her temper? They were chalk and cheese, oil and water. Opposites attracted, she knew, but between them it was a violent attraction that brought more sparks than anything else. If there were any compensations to be had, Verity was not aware of them. Resolutely she pushed to the back of her mind the memory of that brief moment of fusion when it had seemed that their bodies, if not their minds, were capable of forgetting the differences between them.

Ramón kept to his word and absented himself as much as possible during the next few days. It was no secret that he was squiring Isabel Delgado about the countryside. There were any number of knowing glances and murmurs in the village after she had been seen in his company at the nearby casino at Alta Gracia and had attended a concert in Cordoba with him.

'You've missed your chance there, *niña*,' Maria Lopez told Verity with all the familiarity of an old friend, when she called in for some stores. 'Señorita Delgado is on the look-out for a husband.'

'She's welcome to try,' shrugged Verity.

'They're taking bets on how long before she nails him.' Maria's eyes were bright with curiosity. 'Have you heard anything?'

Verity laughed casually. 'Only that she may have a task on her hands, if it's a wedding ring that she wants. He's not the marrying type—he told me.'

'Did he indeed?' The older woman gave her a penetrating look and Verity wondered uncomfortably if she had been indiscreet. 'He confides in you, does he?'

'Hardly,' she said briefly. 'Are those cherries fresh?'

'Of course. They came in yesterday from Mendoza— lovely juicy fruit.' Lost in her selling pitch, Maria was easily diverted from other embarrassing topics, and Verity was relieved.

Her father attacked the same subject that evening.

'Vance not with us tonight?' he enquired, seeing the table laid for two places instead of the now customary three.

'He's out somewhere. He said he'd be back late.' Verity sounded casual. 'It's quite like old times, isn't it, Dad? Just the two of us on our own.'

'Yes. It makes a change. He's out with the fair Isabel, is he? She makes the most of her chances, does that girl.'

'Meaning I don't, I suppose?' she snapped. 'I didn't think that you were as keen for me to find a husband as the Delgados are for Isabel to get herself engaged.'

Mark Williams looked slightly taken aback by the violence of her tone. 'Steady on, love! There's no need to get upset about it. I just meant that she likes to have a good time.'

She really must try to keep a hold on her temper—it seemed to be running away with her these days. 'Sorry, Dad, I didn't think. I didn't mean to fly off the handle.

It's just that——' She broke off, wondering how best to explain matters to him.

'It's just that you're a bit touchy where Vance is concerned.' Her father finished the sentence for her. 'I had noticed. You don't like him very much, do you?'

'I loathe him,' she said shortly, glad that it was out in the open at last. She had not liked pretending in front of her father.

'That's a bit strong.'

She shrugged. 'I can't help it. It's just the way I feel. I think it's mutual.' She knew it was, but she was not going to tell her father that. It might lead to awkward questions.

'I'm sorry,' Mark Williams said simply. 'I like the man.'

'I know. That's why I——' Verity made an expressive gesture with her slim hands. 'There wasn't any point discussing it with you.'

'Not if you feel like that.' He sighed. 'It's a pity, though.'

'Don't tell me you were habouring matchmaking schemes too!'

Her father laughed. 'Acquit me of that. You'll be leaving me soon enough. I've no desire to hasten the process.'

She reached across the table and put her hand over his in a loving grasp. 'Idiot! I'll be with you for a long while yet.' She sighed. 'If only we knew what the future held. Has Ramón Vance said anything to you yet?'

'Has he decided anything, you mean? If he has, he hasn't told me. To tell you the truth, it's rather weighing on me at present. I'd like to get things settled. If it's bad news I'd rather know.'

'He should have seen all he wants to see by now,'

Verity mused. 'He's toured the house and the *potreros*, even the far fields on the eastern boundary. He must have inspected every individual animal we keep. He's talked to all the men the *estancia* employs. He's gone over the farm finance books umpteen times, with and without the bank manager to explain them. What more does the man want?'

'Heaven knows.' Mark Williams sounded a little dispirited. 'I expect he'll tell me in his own good time. But the waiting gets one down rather.'

It must have been harder for him than for her, she thought sympathetically. She only had to put up with the man in the evenings and at breakfast-time. Her father had him as an observer on most working days. His men would know that he was on trial to a certain extent. That could not have been pleasant. But he had made the best of it and had not complained. He was even able to like the man who was imposing all this on him.

'You're nice, Dad,' she told him warmly.

'So are you.' He grinned at her. 'We sound like a mutual admiration society!'

Rather different from her and Ramón, Verity thought wryly. She smiled. 'It'll be even better when everything's sorted out, you'll see. Once that man's off our backs, life will be wonderful!'

They had a foretaste of exactly how wonderful it would be when Ramón announced next day that he would be away for the weekend.

'I hope it won't inconvenience the housekeeping arrangements too much,' he told Verity over dinner. The mockery in his eyes showed her that he knew only too well how happy the news would make her.

'I'll manage, I suppose,' she said ungraciously.

It was left to Mark Williams to ask pleasantly where

he was going. 'Business or pleasure? You work too hard, Vance.'

'A little of both.' He smiled, showing white teeth. It was strange how pleasant he could be to anyone except herself, Verity mused. 'The Delgados have invited me to stay at their weekend place near San Roque. It sounds quite pleasant up there. There's good fishing, and Delgado tells me that he keeps a boat for sailing in good weather. And there are all kinds of sports to be had.'

Among which Isabel Delgado would figure largely, Verity had no doubt. Chaperoned by her family she might be, but there were always ways of dodging supervision, and her mother and father would probably turn a blind eye if they thought marriage was on the cards for their daughter.

She watched him stride out to the Land Rover with a small weekend bag in his hand next afternoon. If she knew Isabel at all the girl would be head over heels in love with him before the two days had elapsed—if she was not in love with him already. What girl wouldn't fall for such a handsome escort, if he put himself out to please her as well? He was wearing a casual safari suit, the jacket unbuttoned to show the tanned expanse of his broad chest, the trousers emphasising his muscled length of leg. He looked all male, Verity had to admit.

He straightened, as if aware that he was being watched, although she had taken care to stand back from the window. 'Verity?'

There was little point in concealing herself. She loosened the catch and opened the window, leaning casually out. 'Yes?'

If he was surprised by her response, he did not show it. He merely studied her with his usual intensity, as if, she always thought, he had to rate her for a prize in a beauty contest and was finding it hard to award her even half a mark. 'I'm leaving now. I'll be back late on Sunday. Tell your father, will you?'

'I'll do that,' she said coolly.

'Will you miss me?' he asked, his tone full of mockery.

'I shouldn't think so.'

'You might be surprised.'

'I might be,' she conceded. 'But I imagine it'll be more like the effect you get when you stop banging your head against a brick wall—a pleasant relief from suffering.'

Ramón left the car and walked up the steps to the verandah. Had he taken offence at the remark? Verity trembled, but held her ground.

'You never miss a chance to hit out at me, do you?' he asked her.

'You could say that I make the most of my opportunities,' she said cautiously. Was he going to make an issue of it?

He was close now, close enough for her to catch a whiff of the tangy aftershave that he was wearing. He must just have bathed and shaved, she registered. Normally, as he was a dark-skinned man, his cheeks showed the beginnings of shadow by this time in the day.

'We're two of a kind, then,' he said softly.

'Are we? Why?'

'I believe in making the most of my opportunities too.'

Before she had time to guess his intention his lips had claimed hers in a long kiss. And the magic was still there between them. He pulled her against him, holding her close, while his mouth continued to plunder hers, fanning a spark of pleasure into a flame that threatened to consume her. They were in full view of anyone coming up the drive to the house, but somehow it did not seem to matter. All that Verity wanted was for the embrace to go on for ever.

Ramón was more in control of himself, and when he released her, prising her clinging arms from him, he looked unmoved except for the glint of satisfaction in his eyes. She could have kicked herself for succumbing so easily. What must he think of her?

'It's a pity we have to use words to communicate, Verity. You and I get on so much better using other methods,' he told her, faintly mocking.

And then he was gone before she had a chance to say anything to him, slamming the car door behind him and giving her an insouciant wave of his hand as he sped down the drive.

She would not miss him, she vowed. She would be only too glad of two clear days away from his irritating presence. But the hours dragged and she caught herself wondering on more than one occasion exactly what was happening in San Roque. She had been there once, staying with some school friends, and she knew the set-up. One spent lazy days basking in the good weather that was almost assured at this time of year. There weren't many sophisticated attractions on offer, just the pleasures of outdoor life.

Ramón would be sailing with Señor Delgado and fishing with him, perhaps—he had mentioned that. But the rest of the time he would be with Isabel. They would walk together by the lake. They would swim, if Isabel could be persuaded to get her bathing suit wet. Or perhaps they would just lie soaking up the sun.

How would Isabel react to the sight of that lithe, bronzed body so close to her own? Would she, like

Verity, feel the first stirrings of desire? Would she give
in to them? The questions chased round and round in
Verity's head even while she tried to keep her mind
firmly on other things. She wasn't really interested,
she told herself. But somehow that didn't stop the process.

Whether she was interested or not, Ramón Vance
did not volunteer much information about the trip
when he returned late on the Sunday evening, looking
rested and relaxed.

'Did you have a good time?' It was left to Mark
Williams to put the polite query. Verity, in the last
stages of clearing the supper table, was ostensibly not
listening.

'Fine, thanks. It made a nice break.' His gaze
flickered over Verity as if she was one of the problems
that he had needed to distance himself from. Then,
quite deliberately it seemed to her, he changed the
subject, talking cattle with her father.

Isabel was more forthcoming when she called two
days later to deliver a book that she claimed she had
promised to lend to Ramón. Verity saw it as a blatant
excuse for her to see the man and took malicious
pleasure in telling the other girl that her quarry had
driven into town for a business discussion.

'He won't be back until quite late, I'm afraid,' she
said, with a noticeable lack of sympathy in her voice.
'I'm so sorry if you've had a wasted journey. You
should have telephoned.'

'It doesn't matter. I hadn't anything else to do.'
Isabel's plump shoulders lifted in a casual shrug.

So much for the idle rich, thought Verity, but did
not say anything. Isabel looked the part, too, her filmy
cotton voile dress in palest lemon swirled expensively
about her, and she was bathed in an overwhelming

cloud of musky French perfume. Verity's nose wrinkled with disgust. She used a fresh floral cologne herself and she found the heavy waves of fragrance rather too much for her. No doubt Ramón Vance would disagree with her. And, to be fair, it had been put on for his benefit alone—of that she was sure.

'Señor Vance will be sorry he missed you,' she volunteered, as silence stretched between them and good manners demanded that she say something.

'Yes,' Isabel agreed smugly.

There was nothing like being assured of one's reception. 'You had a good time together at San Roque?' Verity could have kicked herself for asking the question once it was uttered. It sounded as if she cared what had happened. And she didn't, of course.

'*Estupendo!*' Isabel launched into a long account of their time together. They had been riding. 'Ramón is an expert horseman, you know.' He swam like a fish, but was gallant enough to accommodate his pace to her more limited ability in the water. He had taken her out on the lake in her father's sailing boat for an idyllic afternoon spent alone together. One evening there had been a concert of folk music by the lake side and he had taken her to it. He had been a perfect escort— '*Muy atento, muy cortes.*' Isabel's face glowed at the memory. '*Y muy macho.*' She glanced slyly at Verity as if to stress the point. 'He's all man.'

'I'm glad you enjoyed yourselves,' Verity said stiffly. Inside her something was cold. Ramón had been amusing himself, she told herself. It was hardly likely that he would want what Isabel had to offer him when he could have that sort of thing many times over in Buenos Aires without the need for a wedding ring. And Isabel was too much her father's daughter to give in without blessing from a priest.

Her thoughts were clearly running on those lines. She smoothed back a strand of her thick black hair that had escaped from the severe chignon in which she wore it and preened slightly. 'My father likes Ramón very much,' she confided.

That said it all. Even Isabel, spoilt and indulged as she was, would not bestow her affections without parental approval. Señor Delgado had obviously given her the green light to encourage Ramón. It would appear that the matter was settled if the other party to it gave his approval. And that was a big 'if'.

Isabel had few doubts as to the power of her charms. She subjected Verity to a long consideration of which dress she should wear to delight him when he took her out to dine at a newly opened restaurant outside Córdoba. 'I haven't been there yet. It sounds rather elegant. One wouldn't want to be under-dressed.'

'No, indeed,' Verity muttered, bored. She did not think there was much danger of that.

'Blue, I think. Ramón likes me in blue—he told me so.' Isabel sounded smug. 'A woman should always try to please her man, shouldn't she?'

'Probably.' Verity wanted to say, 'He's not yours yet, so don't count your chickens.' She was surprised by the violence of her reaction to the idea of the two of them together. It was because Isabel deserved better than that, she told herself. Smug and self-satisfied the girl might be, and spoilt and pampered and over-indulged, and a crashing snob into the bargain. But the awakening that she would get when she realised that Ramón Vance could not be twisted round her little finger would be an undeservedly shattering one. If Verity herself had a lot to learn about men, Isabel had even more, for all her two years' advantage, if she was hoping to tame a man like that.

'Your girl-friend called while you were out,' she told him acidly when Ramón returned to the *estancia*, long after Isabel had taken her reluctant leave. Mark Williams was not back yet and Verity had prepared a cold supper and was sitting out on the verandah, enjoying the evening air, so pleasant after the baking heat of the day, when even the *pampas* breezes blew hot air rather than cool.

'Isabel?' He halted before her chair, a dark brow raised in interrogation.

'How many others have you acquired in the neighbourhood in the brief time that you've been here?' She saw a gleam in his eyes and went on hastily, 'No, don't tell me. I don't want to know.'

'Jealous, Verity?'

'Just not interested,' she said coolly.

He shrugged. 'And what did Isabel want?'

'You. With or without a noose through your nose.'

The corners of his firm mouth lifted in something like amusement, although whether at her expense or at Isabel's, Verity could not tell. 'A pity I missed her.'

'That's what she thought. I'm afraid that telling me tales of your cosy weekend together was a good deal less amusing for her than seeing you again.'

'For someone who doesn't give a damn about me, you take a commendable interest in my activities,' he said lazily. 'Was it entertaining hearing?'

'Not in the least,' she snapped.

'You needn't have listened.'

'I wouldn't have done, if there had been any way of stopping her,' she told him sweetly.

'In that case you're not very resourceful.' He eased his powerful frame into the chair beside her and it creaked in protest at his weight.

'I couldn't be rude to the girl.'

'Why not? You don't seem to have any hang-ups about insulting me,' he taxed her.

'You're different,' she muttered.

'So I'd gathered.' He paused a moment, as if waiting for her to enlarge on the statement, and, when she was silent, continued, 'It's a pity that you feel like that.'

'I spoil your record, I suppose.'

'Is that how you really think that I see women?' he asked.

'Don't you? Aren't they just numbers in a little black book designed for your pleasure?'

He seemed amused, not angered by the thought. 'When I was twenty, perhaps. But not any more. I look for more out of a relationship than my own selfish pleasure, I hope. I give as well as take from any woman I befriend.'

'Noble sentiments,' she said with faint sarcasm. 'And what exactly do you give to Isabel?'

'You mean she hasn't told you? And I thought women always spilled all to their best girl-friends.'

'I'm not Isabel's best friend.' Not by a long chalk, Verity thought.

'She must be unusually discreet for one of your sex.' A look of amusement crossed his face.

'You mean you have an understanding with her?' It was a strangely difficult question to ask, for some reason. It shouldn't matter. But somehow it did.

'You could say that.' He stretched lazily like a big cat and turned his face to catch the last rays of the evening sunshine.

'Oh. I see.' So Isabel was right to be so smug; she had captured the prize that she was after. Verity was slightly stunned.

'Do you? I wonder.'

He was watching her keenly, looking for some reaction, she supposed. 'I'm surprised,' she said. 'I thought you weren't the marrying type.'

'I wasn't. But when a man meets his fate, he accepts it.' He gave an expressive shrug. 'If the girl is exactly what you've been looking for all your life, you don't wait around. You grab her before someone else gets to her.'

That sounded certain enough. He knew what he wanted—and he had found that quality in Isabel of all people.

'I suppose outsiders never understand what draws two people together and makes them fall in love.' She voiced her thoughts.

Ramón answered her unspoken question. 'You wonder what I see in her?' He was too perceptive by half, she thought. He considered the horizon with a faintly calculating expression. 'She's restful,' he said at last. 'Isabel isn't a little spitfire like you, Verity, but calm and placid and welcoming. A man likes to come home to a little peace and tranquillity.'

'Is that how you like your women, like milk and water?' Verity asked carefully. It was an effort to sound brightly interested, when, for some strange reason, she wanted to burst into tears. But that would never do. He might think that his news had affected her in some way. 'No wonder we never got on!'

'You're not one of my women, Verity,' he told her with cruel emphasis.

'No.' It was only a whisper. She wondered why his words should hurt quite so much. She roused herself to ask, 'Where will you live?'

'After the marriage, you mean?'

'Yes. Will it be Buenos Aires? I suppose it will, as you've got business there. It'll be a great change for— for——'

'For my wife?' He said the word that she found herself unable to speak. He shrugged. 'If she loves me, she'll adapt to a new lifestyle. You would, wouldn't you?'

'Yes, I think I would,' she said slowly. It would be hard luck on Isabel if she didn't feel inclined to change when the man in her life demanded it. Clearly *he* had no intention of altering his own ways. Marriage would be on Ramón's terms not those of the woman he wed, however much he loved her. Although he hadn't said a word about *that*, Verity noted absently. 'You'll be leaving us soon, then?' She supposed any normal man would be eager for his wedding to take place as soon as could be arranged.

'It won't be long now,' he agreed. 'You'll be glad to see the back of me, I expect.'

'I expect so,' she echoed. Suddenly she didn't know. She didn't know at all. It was what she had wanted for weeks. But now she was not sure.

'I'd better go and ring Isabel.' Ramón got to his feet in one lithe movement and sauntered towards the house. 'Is supper ready yet?'

Normally she would have flared up at this reminder of her duties, but tonight, for some reason, it passed her by. 'It won't be long. Dad should be back shortly.'

'Good. I'm hungry.' He disappeared into the house, leaving the door ajar behind him.

Verity supposed she had better make a move. There were still a couple of things to attend to in the kitchen—fruit to prepare for a dessert and the table to lay. She got slowly to her feet and stood for a moment, gazing unseeingly down the drive. Usually she loved looking at the wide avenue of eucalyptus trees that some previous owner had planted to give style to Vista Hermosa. Green and stately, they always seemed symbolic of the strength and purpose of life on the *pampas*. Tonight she didn't even register their presence. They were of no comfort to her. She turned to go in. Suddenly she felt tired and dispirited.

From inside the house she heard Ramón's deep tones asking someone, probably one of the servants at Los Molinos, for Isabel. As Verity paused in the doorway, reluctant to intrude on a personal conversation, she registered the caressing note that came into his voice as his *novia* came to the phone. It must be love, she thought. He had never talked to *her* in that intimate, special way, as if she was the only person in the world who mattered to him. Isabel must have hidden depths to inspire such devotion.

'Isabel? *Que tal, niña?*' The dark eyes were on Verity, resenting her presence and she hastened to walk past him towards the kitchen regions. She heard him apologising for having missed her visit to Vista Hermosa and promising to see her as soon as he could. Verity wondered if he would go haring round to Los Molinos that very evening, but evidently lover-like ardour did not extend that far. '*Mañana, chica, mañana,*' he was saying firmly as she shut the door behind her to blot out the sound of the conversation.

Mechanically she began to set out cutlery on the table, laying out the pieces with unaccustomed precision, as if her life depended on the neatness of the display. She didn't care, she told herself. Let him talk to Isabel as if he worshipped the ground that she walked on. What difference did it make to her? Ramón meant nothing to her. She hated the man, and had done ever since his arrival.

But Verity knew it was not true. She could be honest with herself, if she refused to acknowledge the fact to others. She was not sorry for Isabel at all. She envied the other girl every moment with Ramón Vance, whether of heaven or hell. And, as the hot tears trickled down her face, Verity admitted the bitter truth that she had been dodging so resolutely for days now; she was in love and the man she loved felt nothing at all for her.

CHAPTER EIGHT

VERITY did not want any supper; food would choke her at the moment. Instead she left the meal ready in the fridge and a note on the table explaining that she felt rotten and had gone to bed. That was certainly true, although her miseries sprang from an altogether different source from the headache that she was feigning.

She cried, stuffing her head deep in a pillow, so that she wouldn't be heard, and then, exhausted, lay dry-eyed and miserable, too wretched to rest. Late in the evening she heard a gentle tap at the door and her father's voice asking, 'Verity, love? Are you all right?' She never suffered from headaches and minor ailments; he was obviously wondering what was wrong with her. But she could not confide in him—not now when it was all so raw and hurtful. Later, perhaps, when the pain had died. If it ever did. Verity did not answer and, as he obviously assumed that she was asleep, she heard his steps fade away along the passage.

How many women had there been in Ramón Vance's past who had gone through exactly the sort of torment that she was suffering now? She should count herself lucky that she had not given him the satisfaction of knowing how she felt about him. All he had ever got from her had been resentment and blazing anger. Not once had she shown him a softer, more caring face.

Except when he had kissed her—then she had not been able to hide her response. Verity burned at the recollection of her wanton behaviour. Did he think less of her because she had told him she hated him, but still melted into his arms every time he had made love to her? Whether he had despised her or not he had seemed ready to take advantage of what she was offering him. But men were like that. They took what they wanted and wasted no time on useless thoughts of self-reproach.

If only life was that simple! But, if you were female, you didn't see things like that. If you loved a man you wanted more than a brief shared physical encounter. You started thinking about commitment, marriage, a home and children, building up a whole lifestyle round the promise offered by a single kiss. Verity allowed herself to think about Ramón's children. They would be sturdy and sure-footed like their father, with dark, solemn faces that could break into charming smiles when they chose. They would be intelligent, too, but without their father's arrogance, his consciousness of his superiority.

She sighed. If she was imagining Ramón as a father, she had better concentrate on Isabel as the mother in the case. It was no use indulging in useless dreams in which she figured as the other parent. She could abandon ideas of a boy and a girl who shared her own chestnut hair and normally happy-go-lucky attitude to life. Perhaps he didn't want children. Perhaps Ramón was the sort of man who wanted his wife to himself, to indulge his whims and fancies, to preside over his dinner parties, impeccably groomed and gowned, helping his career along, without irritating cries from the nursery to distract her attention.

Had they discussed the question, he and Isabel? Had they talked of practical matters, or were they too carried away by the romance of the moment to mention such down-to-earth subjects? Ramón had certainly seemed cool enough about the announcement of his intentions. But she had heard the intimate note in his voice as he had talked to her on the phone. He cared. And Isabel? Who knew what she thought? Ramón was good-looking and he had money enough to support her in a gracious way. In the Delgado household, Verity suspected, other considerations came pretty low on the list of necessities for a happy married life.

'Did you and Mum think about money when you got married?' Verity asked her father the next morning. He was showing an alarming interest in her supposed headache of the night before and, in an effort to divert him, she posed the question that was uppermost in her mind.

He laughed. 'About that and nothing else, I should think. We hadn't two pesos to rub together. There were times when we did get to wondering where our next meal was coming from. We had no families to support us when the going got tough. My parents were dead and your mother's relatives, what there were of them, were back in England.'

'But you were happy, weren't you?' she pressed him. 'Money wasn't everything.'

'It seemed like it sometimes.' Mark Williams shook his head ruefully at the memory. 'Money can't buy you health, but there's precious little else it can't get for you.'

Ramón had once said something similar to her, she recalled. He had said he could buy a wife if he required one. Was that indeed what he had done? But Isabel would be rich in her own right one day when anything happened to her father. She wasn't forced to accept the first eligible man who offered for her. No, it was a case of like attracting like, money attracting money.

'So it would seem,' she agreed, faintly despondent.

'What's the matter, love? Don't tell me you're thinking of marrying a pauper. I was looking to you to restore the family fortunes.'

He could sense her low spirits and, unknowing of their cause, he was doing his best to jolly her out of them. Verity appreciated the attempt and tried to respond to it. Perhaps sharing the news might help?

'Not me,' she said, trying to keep her voice even. 'Ramón.'

'Vance?' Her father queried. 'What do you mean?'

'Hasn't he told you his good tidings yet?'

'I'm not with you. You mean he's getting married? Is this true, Vance?'

Verity started. She turned swiftly and registered the tall figure in the doorway with something like dismay. How long had he been standing there unobserved? Had he heard her asking her father those questions about marriage? Verity did not want him thinking that she cared enough to brood about the matter. His uncanny knack of reading her thoughts might lead him on to other conclusions, however much she protested her indifference to him and the girl of his choice.

He entered the room and sat down at the table beside them. 'How's the invalid?' he asked Verity, ignoring her father's question.

'Fine, thank you,' she hastened to assure him, the words tumbling out in an effort to sound convincing.

'That headache must have come on very suddenly. You seemed all right when we were talking just before supper.' His brown eyes dwelt perhaps a fraction too long on the tell-tale red that still showed round hers and the shadows that indicated a sleepless night.

'It did. It must have been the sun or something,' she lied desperately.

'Or something,' he agreed, and she thought she caught a faintly mocking note in his voice. 'I'm glad you're recovered.'

If only it had been a headache that she had suffered. Verity suspected that what she was really enduring would take a good deal longer to go away.

'Come on, Vance, you're not dodging the issue that easily. Is marriage on the cards for you?' Mark Williams was in a teasing mood, reluctant to abandon the question he had posed. 'Are congratulations in order?'

'I should save them yet awhile. The lady hasn't said yes.'

'Don't tell me you're having a hard time persuading her, whoever she is. That I can't believe.' Mark Williams voiced his amazement.

Verity couldn't understand it either, although she remained silent about it. What was the matter with Isabel? Didn't she know that she had been offered a chance that most women would grab at with both hands? Was she really prepared to put Ramón through the old courtship game of three proposals before she consented to marry him? That went out with the Dark Ages, Verity thought.

Perhaps her father had raised some objection. But it hardly seemed likely in the light of all those approving glances that Verity had seen herself at the dinner party they had attended. Whatever the case, Isabel had better hurry up. A man like Ramón might grow tired of waiting for an answer and look elsewhere. What a fool that girl was! Either that or she was very certain of him. And how sure could any woman be of a man like him?

Amazingly Ramón laughed. If his male ego had been dented by a refusal, he showed no sign of it. 'Women take time to make up their minds. They take an age to choose a dress. Picking a partner for life should take a little longer, I suppose.'

'Yes, it's a female prerogative to make the man wait on every occasion,' Mark Williams agreed. 'Goodness knows I wasted quite a bit of time hanging around for Verity's mother. Not that she wasn't worth it,' he added hastily, meeting his daughter's reproachful eyes. 'If your wife-to-be makes you as happy as Ann made me, you'll be a lucky man and no mistake.'

'I intend to be,' Ramón said smoothly.

'Happiness doesn't come to order. You have to work at it.'

A dark brow raised politely, but quizzically in her direction made Verity wish she had not volunteered that particular piece of worldly wisdom. It sounded naïve and childish. How often had he told her she had a lot to learn about the world? And here she was presuming to teach him.

'Perhaps,' he conceded. 'Sometimes it's just a bonus from the gods. The important thing is not to pass it by.'

'I hope you don't,' she told him, thinking that he would be blessed indeed if he achieved instant bliss with Isabel.

'I usually seize my opportunities, Verity.' His eyes scanned her face, resting for an instant on her full mouth in a deliberate reminder of one occasion at least when he had done exactly that.

If he wanted to silence her, he had achieved his aim. Verity lowered her gaze, finding the tablecloth of sudden, absorbing interest. Why was it that he could outpoint her so easily in these verbal battles?

If Mark Williams sensed an uncomfortable break in the conversation, he gave no hint of it. 'Well, you'll let us know when we can wish you happy, won't you?' he said cheerfully. 'It'll certainly call for a celebration drink.'

'You're very kind.' There was genuine warmth in the other man's reply. 'But I think there'll be more immediate matters to toast than my impending marriage.'

'Verity told you about her birthday, did she? Yes. Nineteen next week. And it seems only yesterday that I was driving to the hospital to fetch her and her mother home for the first time. Do you know——'

'Dad!' Verity protested, embarrassed. 'Ramón doesn't want to hear about that. Don't bore him.'

Her father laughed. 'Yes, you're right, of course. Parenthood,' he said. 'It takes you like that. You'll know how it is when you've a family of your own, Vance. A word of encouragement and out come the photographs. You can't keep a proud father down.'

'No, I imagine not.' He sounded amused, but sympathetic. 'Nineteen, are you, Verity? Such a great age!'

He was mocking her again and she looked resentfully at him. It wasn't her fault that she was so young. And nineteen wasn't that youthful, after all. She was old enough to drive a car, to vote, to work for her living. Many girls of her age were married with a family of two or more children. A couple of her classmates from school had graduated straight from the classroom to looking after their own homes. They were mature adults and accepted as such. And so was she. There was no need to treat her the way he did.

'At least I can still look forward to my birthdays,' she said with spirit.

'If that's a dig at me, young lady, as I suspect it is——' her father intervened before Ramón could reply.

She turned to smile at him, her anger momentarily forgotten and mischief dancing her eyes. 'Never mind,

Dad. You're young at heart.'

'Cheek,' he said, but he laughed. 'What would you do with her?' he appealed to the other man.

Ramón shook his head and declined to offer an answer, although the glint in his eye suggested that he could have come up with any number of solutions that would have appealed to him. She suspected there were times when he would like nothing better than to put her over his knee and spank her. That was one opportunity she never intended to offer him.

'I wasn't talking about birthdays, in fact.' Their visitor broached the subject again when Mark Williams' mirth had subsided. 'I had something else in mind.'

'Oh?' The older man was suddenly all attention. 'You can't mean—you're not saying it's good news about—about——'

Kind for once, Ramón Vance helped him out. 'About Vista Hermosa. Yes.' He smiled and Verity, hanging on his words, registered the magnetic pull that he always had for her. 'At least, I hope you'll think so.'

After he had outlined his plans for the *estancia*'s future Verity and her father sat reeling under the shock. Things were certainly going to be different from now on, if Ramón had his way. And, as the owners had given him carte blanche to organise matters, it seemed as if he would indeed bring about drastic changes.

'I can't believe it,' Mark Williams kept repeating. 'It's what's been needed all along, of course—an injection of funds into the place in order to get it back to where it was before matters started going downhill. With more staff and more equipment it shouldn't be long before things are looking up again.'

'I hope so.' For the first time a slightly grim note came into Ramón's eyes. 'I'm giving you all the help I

can in every practical way, Williams. But in the last
analysis it all rests with you. If you make a go of it,
that's fine. If you don't, there won't be any more
chances for you.'

'I realise that. And it's good of you to trust me to
make the improvements. I won't let you down.'

'If you'd come to the company earlier and explained
that you needed help instead of keeping it to yourself
for all this time, matters would have taken less sorting
out, less mental anguish all round.' Ramón glanced
briefly at Verity as he spoke. 'But that's water under
the bridge now, I suppose.' He held out his hand to
the older man. 'We'll sort out the details later and I'll
go through the financial arrangements with you. But,
in the meantime, consider the affair settled.'

Mark Williams grasped him firmly. 'You're a good
man, Vance. I appreciate what you're offering me. And
you've my word that I'll do my best for you.'

There was a moment of emotion-filled silence and
then he came over to Verity and hugged her. 'Do you
hear that, love? It's going to be all right after all.'

She smiled at him rather mistily, relief at the news
rather overwhelming her. 'It's great, Dad. But I told
you it would all turn out for the best, didn't I? Perhaps
you'll listen to me next time.'

'There isn't going to be a next time,' Mark Williams
said buoyantly. 'It's success all the way from now on.
We'll even give Delgado a run for his money, if he
likes.' He glanced over at Ramón. 'Can I go and tell
the men? They've been worried too. It's their liveli-
hood, and some of them have been at Vista Hermosa
longer than I have.'

'Go ahead,' Ramón nodded his assent. 'They'd
probably prefer to hear the news from you anyway.'

'Dad, you haven't had any breakfast yet,' Verity

called after him, and sighed as she heard the yard door bang behind him.

'He's got more important things on his mind just now.'

'I suppose so.' She gave him a wary look. 'It is true, isn't it? Dad's job is secure?'

'I thought we'd just established that,' he said lazily. 'Or weren't you listening?'

'Yes, but——'

'But you still don't trust me, do you?'

'I don't know what to make of you,' she said honestly. 'If it's all going ahead as you've just told us, then it's marvellous news. But——'

'But?' he prompted.

'I've got a strong feeling there's a fly in the ointment somewhere. You're being very generous——'

'I can afford to be. It's not my money. It's coming from the consortium's pockets. It's relatively simple to be open-handed with someone else's money,' he told her.

'I didn't mean the money.'

'What then?'

She shrugged. 'I didn't think you'd let Dad keep control. I thought that you'd put a younger man in. It's what most people in your position would have done.'

'You're very shrewd,' he drawled.

'And you're very devious,' she snapped. 'And I don't trust you an inch whatever my father may think about you.'

'Your father's got his head screwed on when it comes to judging character. And he's got a good few years' start on you.'

'I follow my instincts, not anything else when I'm making up my mind about people.'

'It's a pity they lead you astray so often,' Ramón commented tersely.

'I don't think they do.'

'Then you're a little fool,' he said pleasantly, getting to his feet.

'Because I disagree with you, I suppose?'

'Because you don't have the honesty to admit it to yourself when you're wrong about something or someone. But that's your problem.' He walked to the door. 'I'd better go and find your father—we've things to discuss. Oh, and Verity——'

'Yes?'

'About that fly in the ointment that you mentioned——'

So she had been right. 'Well?' she asked him.

'You were right when you suspected I might put a younger man in. But in a supervisory capacity only. Your father's perfectly capable of running the place, but he needs a little support and advice. And I intend to see that he gets it.'

There was a sudden cold feeling at the back of her neck. Verity was suddenly certain of what was coming next. 'You're going to be keeping in close touch from Buenos Aires?' she hazarded.

'I shall be around here for a while yet to see the start of the improvement operation. And then, if it all seems to be going according to plan, I'll be back every weekend to keep everything on the right track.'

Her face must have shown how appalling she found the prospect. 'What about your other work? How will you manage?'

'I think you can safely leave that to me to worry about, don't you?' he rebuked her. 'And I'm sure your father will welcome the idea even if you don't. Try to think of somebody besides yourself for a change, Verity.'

On that disagreeable note he left her. He hadn't had any breakfast either, but she wasn't going running after him. He could starve as far as she was concerned, Verity told herself. She poured herself a cup of coffee and sat down at the table, cradling the cup absently in her hands while she attempted to sort out the muddle that her thoughts were in.

It was good news about Vista Hermosa. Whatever Ramón said, she was glad for her father's sake as much for her own that the only home that they had known was not to be taken from them. But the prospect of Ramón's continual presence about the place was an entirely different matter. She could bear the fact that she was in love with him. She could bear the fact that he intended to marry someone else—just, and only just. Given time she might even get over him one day. But not if he was constantly under her nose.

Now that matters were settled and her father's job was safe, she supposed she could look forward to university and her trip back to her parents' homeland. But that wouldn't be for a while yet. How could she exist in the meantime, eating her heart out for a man who cared nothing for her and resenting the girl he would be courting in her place? Verity felt ill at the thought.

At least he did not know her secret. She had that consolation. Nobody did, not even her father, from whom she had never kept any important matter in her life. This was her problem and it would remain entirely hers to solve as best she could. Outwardly she made every effort to share Mark Williams' enthusiasm over the news of their reprieve. She listened patiently while he detailed every change to be made, every new piece of equipment that was to be bought once the money was available at the bank.

'We're taking on another ten men initially. We'll see how it goes with them. We may get a few more on a temporary basis later,' he told her. Already, she noticed, he was talking as if he and Ramón were a team. He showed no resentment of the other man—if anything he seemed almost glad that the decision making was to be a dual responsibility in future. 'I feel like a new man,' he said, when she cautioned him about overdoing it. 'I've got a sense of purpose again. It's wonderful!'

'Yes, it is,' she agreed. It was ages since she had seen him so happy about his work. She was grateful to Ramón for that at least and, making an effort, she told him so.

It was evening, the light fading fast over the flat landscape, as he stood on the edge of the verandah, gazing out into the distance. Verity wondered if he was expecting Isabel to drive over from Los Molinos. She had heard him fixing something with the other girl over the phone. She had not intended to listen, but somehow she couldn't help herself. In a strange way she almost enjoyed tormenting herself with the knowledge of his involvement with Isabel. It was as if, by reminding herself of the fact, her own feelings became more bitter-sweet.

She realised when he turned and she saw that he was still in working clothes that he could hardly be waiting for Isabel. She would expect him to be immaculately dressed for her benefit. Outward appearances mattered overmuch to her. Clothes didn't make the man. Although, looking at Ramón now, Verity could have been fooled by his appearance into thinking him a true man of the *pampas*. Dark jeans clung to his long powerful legs and the shirt that he wore emphasised his breadth of shoulder. At his waist was belted the *rastra*, the traditional *gaucho* belt, ornamented with silver coins and studs, and his tattered leather jerkin was tossed aside on a chair next to him, along with the slouch hat that he wore to keep off the blazing force of the midday sun.

He swung round at her approach and an impatient look crossed his face when he realised who it was. 'Does your father want me?' he asked, preparing to head indoors.

'No.' She could hardly blame him for assuming that she was a reluctant message-bearer. She had not sought him out on her own behalf for a long time. 'I wanted to speak to you.'

'Go ahead.' He leaned back against the post of the verandah, one booted leg resting against the chair. 'What's the problem?'

He assumed it wasn't a social encounter. He was right, she supposed. Verity was silent for a moment, wondering how to begin. He was not being exactly encouraging. But she probably deserved that.

'I wanted to thank you,' she said baldly at last.

'For what?' He looked taken aback, or as much as *he* ever could be.

'For helping Dad, for giving him this chance. I don't know if you realised what Vista Hermosa meant to him. I don't think he did until there was a possibility that someone might take it all away from him. Since you gave him the good news he's taken on a new lease of life. You said I was selfish and I didn't care about him, but I do. And I just wanted you to know that.'

Having said her piece, she prepared to leave him, but he stopped her by the simple means of reaching out a hand and grasping her arm. The feel of his fingers against her bare arm sent a ripple of sensation through her and she forced herself to stay calm. He's not interested in you, she told herself. Forget it.

'I'm glad you think I can do something right,' he said. 'It makes a refreshing change.'

'I haven't altered my opinion of you overall.'

'Oh, hardly that,' he mocked her. 'Tell me, Verity, how long are you going to cling to that vision of me as a bold, bad beast seeking to devour you?'

'For as long as I believe it to be true.'

'And there's nothing that I can do to convince you that my intentions are entirely honourable?'

He was stroking her forearm now, his touch tantalisingly light against her skin, deliberately seeking a reaction from her.

'Save your pretty speeches for Isabel,' she advised him. 'She might appreciate them—I don't.'

'Most women like pretty speeches,' he said. 'You're the exception. You prefer actions to words, don't you?'

She should have tried to get away, but some force held her fast, rooted to the spot. She breathed a little faster as he captured her hand and raised it to his mouth, nibbling the soft skin of her palm. 'You like this, don't you?' he asked her.

'No,' she lied.

'Then tell me to stop.'

She didn't want him to. Her lips moved to protest, but no sound emerged. He pulled her closer to him, his hands caressing her as he did so, stroking the supple length of her spine and sending shivers through her as she reacted to his touch.

'Look at me, Verity,' he insisted and, when she tried to turn her head away from him, scared that he would see the telltale feeling in her face and interpret it correctly, he put a hand under her chin and forced her to obey him. Surely he must see how much she cared. It must be shining out of her face, that mixture of love and desire, combined with a reluctance to admit her need of him.

Whatever he saw seemed to satisfy him. Before his lips claimed hers she saw a flicker of expression in his usually impassive features. Sometimes he seemed to put a deliberate guard on his feelings where she was concerned. Now it was stripped away and she could see desire flame on his face. He wanted her as much as she wanted him—there was no doubt of that.

His kiss roused her to fever pitch, his touch sent a thousand new sensations flooding through her. If she lived to be a hundred, Verity thought, no man would ever excite her like this one. He made her feel all woman, passionate and turbulent with emotions. Verity was lost to the outside world, living only for the feel of his body against hers, the firm pressure of his thigh, the strong beat of his heart against her breast, the roughness of his cheek as it brushed hers.

She could never have called a halt. But Ramón did, pushing her from him with firm insistence.

'No!' she protested, and tried to push back into his arms, seeking the warmth and passion that they had shared.

'No,' he echoed, but he meant something different. He was rejecting her.

Realisation hit her like a douche of cold water when she heard his muttered expletive and felt him step away from her. She felt cheap and used. 'All right,' she said with effort. 'I think you proved your point success-fully.'

He was breathing faster than usual, she noticed. Perhaps he wasn't as much in control of himself as he imagined. 'I wasn't trying to prove anything,' he said. 'Believe that, Verity.'

She gave a laugh that just missed being a sob. 'How can I?'

'You go to a man's head. I couldn't help myself.'

Was that intended as an apology? Was he sorry he had kissed her? She didn't know what he meant. Suddenly she felt tired of fencing with the man, tired of wondering what made him tick.

'I'm sorry,' she said, but she didn't know why. She supposed that it was a plea for understanding, a regret that things between them had not gone differently, that they hadn't been friends.

'Don't be,' he told her. 'It'll come right in the end.'

But happy endings were the stuff of fairy stories not of real life, Verity thought as she drifted off to sleep later that night. If only life was as cut and dried as that, with villains defeated and heroes triumphing and everyone getting their just deserts. She fell into a troubled dream in which Isabel, clad in spotless white, her dark hair secured in a medieval headdress, lured Ramón away from her. 'He's going to fight *my* dragons for me,' she said, her face gloating with pleasure at her triumph over Verity. 'Find your own man. This one's mine.' And, even in her dream, Verity was conscious of an overwhelming sense of loss.

CHAPTER NINE

VERITY was awake early on the morning of her birthday. It was a habit that stretched back to childhood when first light had always revealed a heap of interesting packages by the foot of her bed to be opened and gloated over in relative silence until a reasonable time had elapsed and she could go and safely wake her parents to share in the thrill of it all.

She remembered the time when she had begged for a pony of her own. She had been six then. Or was it seven? She had woken up to hear a snuffling sound and see a shaggy brown head scrabbling at the flimsy window screen. For a terrified instant she had retreated under the cover of the bedclothes, until curiosity had got the better of fear and she had emerged to recognise what it was and had gone over to make friends. How her parents had laughed when she had told them the story!

Those times were past now, as were her youthful shrieks of glee at discovering exactly the presents that she wanted and had been hinting at for weeks beforehand. Since her mother had died a lot of the joy had gone out of the family times that they had always made so much of. Christmas, birthdays and anniversary occasions came and went without the same happiness that used to surround them.

Her father tried his best, of course. But it wasn't the same. He knew it and so did Verity. And this year she was even more aware of the fact that the thing that she had set her heart on, the one present that would bring her happiness, was completely beyond her father's power to obtain for her. There was no way that anyone could hand her Ramón Vance's love, tied with a silk bow and with a card saying, 'For Verity, for a lifetime'. It couldn't happen, however much she wanted it.

She sighed heavily. This wasn't going to be a special day. It wouldn't be particularly happy. If Ramón chose to take himself off with Isabel, she would spend the time brooding. If he stayed at the *estancia*, there was a fair chance that there would be heated words between them. She had a very low boiling point where he was concerned and, unable to tell him that she loved him, she found herself going to the opposite extreme and doing everything in her power to demonstrate how little she cared if she provoked him.

Perhaps it would be a normal working day for everyone. Usually her father made every effort to spend the entire day with her. 'Birthdays are special,' he said. 'Work comes a long way second.' She had been assuming it would be the same this year, whatever the problems at Vista Hermosa. But perhaps Ramón wouldn't see things that way. Her father wasn't really his own master any more. He jumped at Ramón's command. And she couldn't see *him* halting ranch business just because a slip of a girl that he didn't particularly like was one year older.

There was a tap at the door. 'Verity? Are you awake?' Her father's head appeared.

'At six o'clock on my birthday morning? I've been awake for ages,' she told him indignantly. 'Come in, Dad.'

'I've brought you a cup of tea.' He brought the tray to her bedside and set it down. He had made it *gaucho*-style, strong *yerba maté*, brewed in silver gourds with small silver straws through which the hot, slightly bitter brew was drunk. 'Happy birthday, love.' He bent over to kiss her and hugged her to him. 'May you have many more, and may all of them be happy ones.'

'Thanks, Dad,' Verity smiled up at him.

'I'm sorry there hasn't been time to go shopping,' he said apologetically. 'You know what the last few days have been like. I haven't known whether I've been coming or going, what with taking on new staff and seeing reps about improvements to the place——'

'Stop worrying—it doesn't matter. I'm a big girl now, too old for heaps of presents,' she reassured him, although she was conscious of a faint feeling of disappointment.

'You deserve a mountain of presents, love. You've been a marvel these last weeks. I don't know what I'd have done without you, and that's the truth. Anyway, here's your card and a little something besides.' He handed her an envelope.

Verity opened it and smiled at the humorous message that he had chosen, ignoring for the moment the other piece of paper that slipped on to the sheet beside her.

'Hey, don't lose that,' Mark Williams cautioned, and she picked it up quickly.

'A cheque?' She noted how much it was for and raised anxious eyes to him. 'Dad, can you afford it?'

'What kind of thank-you is that?' he teased her. 'Yes, I can afford it now. Vance has given me a pay rise too. Now that my job's secure it looks as if I'll be able to put a bit on one side for the first time in my life.'

'Not if you waste it on me, you won't,' Verity told him. 'This is a small fortune.'

'I think you'll find it vanishes pretty rapidly when you get round to spending it. And it's about time that you splashed out a bit and got yourself some new clothes. It's the sort of thing that your mother would have attended to, if she'd been with us. She wouldn't want to see you looking dowdy.'

'Do you think I am?' Verity didn't think her father ever really noticed what she was wearing. Like most men, he took female dress pretty well for granted unless stunned by something that was completely out of the ordinary.

'To tell you the truth, I hadn't thought much about it,' Mark Williams confirmed her thought. 'It was Vance who said something to me.'

Verity's face flamed in sudden humiliation. 'I suppose I must seem a bit homespun after the women he meets in everyday life. But I didn't think I was that bad.'

The hurt must have registered in her voice, because her father glanced at her in concern. 'I'm putting it badly, Verity. It wasn't like that at all. He just pointed out that you were growing up fast. You weren't a child any more, but a young lady. And young women like to dress up occasionally.'

'I've nothing to dress up for,' Verity said. 'Jeans and blouses are what suit me best, and they're practical wear for the *estancia*. Unlike dear Isabel Delgado, I can count the number of social events I attend in a year on the fingers of one hand.'

'That'll change too, now that the ranch is taking on a new lease of life. There'll be times when I'll be entertaining, and I hope you'll act as hostess for me. At least until you leave home. And you enjoy new clothes—all women do.' Her father sounded slightly pained by her reception of his gift. 'I thought you'd be pleased.'

What a churlish beast she was! Just because the gesture had been prompted by Ramón there was no reason to throw it back in her father's face. He thought it would make her happy. He had seized upon the idea once Ramón had put it to him. Verity forced a happy expression to her face. 'Of course I'm pleased—just a bit taken aback, that's all. And I'll enjoy spending it. You're right, you know. You'll be surprised just how frivolous I can be when the mood takes me. I can be as extravagant as the next girl when it comes to re-stocking my wardrobe.'

'That's my girl!' Mark Williams looked relieved. 'You can take the car into Córdoba today. Have a splurge while you're in the mood, otherwise you won't feel as if you've had a birthday.'

Obviously he was going to be engaged elsewhere. Verity swallowed her disappointment and her childish urge to say, 'But I want to be with you.' She was not a child any longer. She was an adult, and grown women didn't give way to impulses like that. 'That would be nice,' she agreed instead, and saw from his expression that she had said the right thing. 'I'll go straight after breakfast. Are you sure you can spare the car?'

'We've another one now, besides Vance's Land Rover,' Mark Williams reminded her of the recent purchase of another ranch vehicle. 'You'll be all right on your own, won't you?'

'Fine,' she assured him. 'It's ages since I've driven, for all I passed my test first time a year ago. It'll be great to get some practice at the wheel.'

'You'll be careful?'

'I'll be careful, Dad. When am I anything else?' she asked him teasingly.

She could have supplied the answer herself, she thought, as she lay back in bed after her father had left her, sipping her tea and brooding. She had tried her best to remain unaffected by Ramón Vance's presence.

But somehow he had got under her guard. She had been stupid enough to let him. And now, when it was too late to remain unhurt, she suddenly realised how careless she had been. But love was like that. It crept up on one unawares and left one feeling totally vulnerable.

She didn't feel in a birthday mood at all, she thought, as she pulled on her pink dress after she had bathed herself. She felt rather flat and dull. Perhaps her father was right, and shopping in Córdoba would restore her spirits. Anything would be better than mooning round the house feeling sorry for herself. She glanced at her dress and accepted another unpalatable truth. Ramón was right about her clothes. She supposed she'd been aware of it for some time, without feeling any great need to do anything about it. And when she had thought about it recently she hadn't liked to bother her father with demands for money. He had had enough problems to contend with.

When she entered the kitchen, prepared to get breakfast ready as usual, she found her father already busy there.

'Out!' he commanded. 'It's my turn today. I'll probably burn the lot, but you're having a rest from cooking for the day. Go and sit down.'

Touched by his thoughtfulness, she obeyed him. There was a small vase of flowers by her place, and she bent down to smell them appreciatively.

'It would have been a large bouquet if the flower shops of the Calle Florida had been a little nearer. In Buenos Aires you can be out to buy flowers before breakfast and get them freshly picked.'

So they were Ramón's contribution. She wouldn't be ungracious about it. 'Thank you,' she said briefly. 'They're very nice.'

If he registered the cool politeness in her tone, he didn't show it. 'I'm glad you like them. But they're only instead of a birthday card. Here's your present.' He held out a small, neatly-wrapped package. 'Go on, take it,' he said as she hesitated. 'It's no use to me.'

There were better ways of offering someone a gift, Verity thought indignantly. But, if that was how he wanted to play it, she would oblige him. 'Thank you. You're very kind.' She took the present and put it by the side of her plate. It felt like a small box and her fingers itched to open it. But a sudden desire to show that she was totally indifferent both to him and to his presents made her leave it there. That would prove something to him.

'Aren't you going to look at it?' She thought she could detect a note of pique in his voice.

'After breakfast,' she said calmly.

'Please yourself,' he shrugged, but she could tell that the gesture had annoyed him. Strangely enough she didn't feel as triumphant as she expected, just rather petty.

Breakfast, under her father's direction, was less palatable than usual. He had, as he had threatened, managed to burn the toast and the coffee was slightly bitter from being percolated too long. But these mishaps served only to lighten the atmosphere as Verity forgot her feelings against Ramón and joined him in teasing the older man about his shortcomings as a cook.

'You're determined to make my birthday a day to remember,' she told her father with mock horror. 'The day I went down with food poisoning, thanks to your cooking!'

Ramón tackled a steak that was overdone at one end and slightly underdone at the other. 'Let's hope the housekeeper that's coming will manage better than this. You did say that she could cook, didn't you, Williams?'

'Housekeeper?' Verity queried blankly. No one had mentioned a housekeeper to her.

'This place is too much for a slip of a girl to try to run,' Ramón told her arrogantly.

'I think I've managed pretty well so far,' she retorted, stung by his assumption that she couldn't cope.

'Managing isn't what's needed, Verity, and you know it. With a house this size you need to be in control, completely on top of everything. And you're not, are you? Admit it.'

She wanted to argue, but she couldn't. He was right, damn him; he was always right. She was getting tired of it.

'Ramón's only trying to lift your load a little, love.' Her father added his comment.

'Oh, is that it? I thought he was just telling me that I'd become redundant about the place,' she said angrily. 'I'm sorry if I didn't understand him properly.'

She heard Ramón give an impatient sigh. 'There's no need to jump to hasty conclusions.'

'Is that what I'm doing?' she challenged him.

'It looks rather like it to me.'

'Calm down, love!' Her father could see the upset behind the show of temper. 'No one's trying to replace you. But now that there's more money available and we can have more staff, it makes sense to have help in the house. We've fixed for a permanent live-in housekeeper and a couple of maids to help out on a day-to-day basis. The place should soon be looking spick and span again, the way it used to be, Verity, when your mother was alive.'

'I suppose it makes sense,' she said grudgingly. 'If you put it like that.'

'Of course it's the right thing to do.' Ramón said impatiently. 'What did you think was going to happen when your father was left on his own, without you to do any work about the house? Or were you planning to battle on in your own sweet way for ever more? You weren't cut out to be a drudge, Verity.'

There were two ways of taking that remark. Verity was sure that he meant the uncomplimentary one. She wasn't any good in the house, just as she wasn't any good in any sphere that he considered womanly. She didn't dress well either. She couldn't make sophisticated conversation. She wasn't a flirt. And she dreaded to think how he rated her performance in making love. Enthusiastic, but totally lacking in skill, she supposed, or words to that effect. Verity glowered resentfully at him.

'You needn't worry, there'll still be plenty for you to do,' he told her kindly.

'And you'll have more time to yourself, love. I've felt guilty about you. You should be enjoying yourself a bit more while you're young, instead of wearing yourself out on housework.' Mark Williams was trying to coax her out of her obvious bad humour.

More time to sit and brood about Ramón Vance. More time to feel inadequate about herself. She wasn't sure that she wanted that. But whether she wanted it or not, it appeared to be all settled. She would have to make the best of it. Clearly she wasn't going to alter matters by protesting. 'It'll be nice to get the place properly to rights again,' she agreed, and saw her father's smile of approval. She could tell from Ramón's quizzical look at her that he wasn't entirely convinced

about her sudden capitulation. She seethed. She was
fed up with the way he just walked in and took over.
Her father might enjoy the experience, but she certainly didn't.

Was it possible to love a man and hate him at the
same time? Verity pondered the problem after the meal
was over and the men had left the room. How could
she resent Ramón so fiercely, yet still ache for a smile
or a sign of tenderness from him? It wasn't logical.
But she supposed love hadn't much to do with that. It
was a madness that seized one and tossed one about,
incapable of rationalising the situation. She just wished
she had managed to steer clear of it.

She pushed her plate aside and saw the small parcel,
half hidden by it. Ramón's present. She had forgotten
it in her wave of outraged feelings. She reached for it
now and opened it, ripping off the paper with sudden
eagerness. There was a box inside, as she had supposed
when she felt it earlier, and it bore the name of the
most exclusive jeweller in Córdoba. Lifting up the lid,
Verity parted the protecting fluff of cotton wool, to
reveal a beautifully dainty pendant. It was silver, she
thought, as was the chain on which it hung. It was a
thistle, exquisitely designed and executed, the petals of
the flower delicate in contrast to the sturdy spikiness
of the stem. She caught her breath in pleasure.

'It reminded me of you.' She started nervously as
Ramón's voice sounded just behind her. She thought
he had left the house, but he must have come back for
something. And now he had caught her mooning over
his present like a lovesick girl. But that was what she
was, wasn't it?

'I always think of the thistle as the flower of the
pampas. In some places it's the only thing that'll grow,
because the climate's so extreme and the landscape's

so exposed. It's stubborn and it's prickly and it soldiers on regardless. And, when it flowers, it's beautiful.' Ramón's explanation continued.

'But I'm not beautiful.' Womanlike, she concentrated on the last part of his remarks.

'You haven't flowered yet.' He sounded faintly amused.

She swung round to confront him, the pendant in her hand. 'Do you think that I'm going to?'

'I'm sure of it.' He was looking at her appraisingly. Was he comparing her with Isabel's smooth, controlled beauty?

'Is that why I'm being despatched to Córdoba to buy myself some new clothes?' she asked him. 'I understand from my father that you think that I'm shabby.'

'I didn't say that. But I suppose I can rely on you to assume that I did.'

'What *did* you say?'

'Does it matter?'

'Not much,' she said carelessly, knowing that it did.

'I said you were an attractive girl who, with a little help, could be an attractive woman. Are you going to take offence at that?'

'How can I? Coming from an expert such as yourself I should take it as a compliment.'

'Most women would,' he agreed. 'But you can turn anything round so that it supports your own warped viewpoint.'

'That's not fair!'

'Isn't it? Think about it some time. You might concede that I'm right. If you can face up to the fact, that is.'

'I can face up to anything,' she told him defiantly, and knew that it wasn't true, even as she spoke the words. She couldn't really face the fact that she loved him, couldn't come to terms with it. But she wasn't going to tell him *that*.

'How about thanking me for the present, then?'

She looked down at the pendant that she was still clutching like a talisman in her hand. The silver thistle was digging into her skin and it was hurting, she realised suddenly. She hadn't noticed until now.

'Thank you,' she muttered.

'Can't you do better than that?'

'What do you want?' Unwisely she raised her face to his and saw exactly what he was expecting from her mirrored in his eyes. She couldn't kiss him, she told herself. She couldn't bear to touch him. It would be too much for her. The feel of his mouth against hers would spark off too many memories, light too many stoked fires. But Ramón was waiting. He would act if she didn't. Reluctantly she reached up and brushed her lips against his tanned cheek. 'Thank you for my present,' she whispered, suddenly breathless.

'You sound like a little girl.' He made no attempt to pull her into his arms and, perversely, she was disappointed.

'Isn't that how you think of me?'

'Sometimes,' he agreed.

'One day you'll take me seriously,' she vowed to him.

'Who says I don't already?' The brown eyes were suddenly serious.

Verity shrugged. His manner never gave much indication of it.

'Shall I put that on for you?' Ramón indicated the pendant.

So that she could feel the touch of his fingers against the bare nape of her neck? So that sensation would flood down her spine, pulsing deliciously through her entire body? And then what would happen? She knew only too well the effect that he had upon her, and it was a danger that she had no intention of courting.

'No, thank you. I don't want to wear it.' She moved away to put it back in its box and shut the lid with a snap.

'Please yourself,' he said. He turned abruptly and made for the door. 'See that you're back in reasonable time from Córdoba, won't you? I don't want you driving at dusk. It's dangerous.'

He spoke out of concern for her welfare, she was sure, but she felt her hackles rise nevertheless. He expected her to obey just because *he* was giving the orders. Did he have to make everything sound like an army command? And, what was worse, he hadn't even waited for her answer, but had disappeared through the door. People didn't disobey Ramón Vance and he didn't expect them to.

But the bad mood faded as she drove out along the drive and turned into the main road. It was a glorious day and somehow she could not be at odds with the world. Ramón and the problems that he caused her were left far behind at Vista Hermosa as she put her foot down on the accelerator and the car ate up the miles between the ranch and Córdoba. This time there was no dark figure sharing the front seat and inhibiting her by his presence. She could please herself. There was no one to criticise her actions or to overrule them.

She made good time, even allowing for a brief stop along the road at a transport café to rest and refresh her parched throat with some cold orange juice. It was nearly lunchtime when she swung triumphantly into the city and parked not far from the bus station. Ramón had negotiated the traffic with his usual competence, unworried by narrow streets and aggressive fellow motorists, but Verity took the coward's way out. It would be easier driving out of town, too, she excused herself.

She locked the car and walked briskly to the area off the Avenida General Paz where, in a pedestrian precinct, all the city's most interesting shops were situated. She stopped at a pavement café to grab a uick bite to eat, a *bocadillo*, made from fresh crusty bread filled with cheese and meat, and a long, cool drink. She timed things well, finishing long before the office crowds spilled out around two o'clock, making it almost impossible to get served rapidly. As she ate she planned her purchases, comparing the mental list she had made of what she needed with the shops that she knew best. Then, having paid the bill, she set off again.

There wasn't a great deal of time. She would have to leave reasonably early, if, in accordance with Ramón's instructions, she wanted to get back before the light went. That was the time when there were most road accidents, when the dusk cloaked objects in a sort of haze and made it difficult to judge distances and speeds of approaching vehicles. Verity allowed herself three hours and no more.

She enjoyed herself. As she went from one small boutique to another she was conscious of her spirits lifting. She hadn't felt this carefree since long before Ramón Vance appeared on the scene. It was good to relax for once. And choosing new clothes was a joy that could rapidly become an addiction, she realised as time went on.

It was a pity that she had no girl friend with her to consult about her choices and to giggle with over some of the extremes of fashion that were displayed. If she had had more notice, she supposed that she would have contacted one of her old school friends who lived nearby. But it didn't really matter. Verity had a good eye for colours and she knew what suited her, and before long she had a pile of bags and parcels attesting to her enthusiasm for the task.

She had cashed the cheque that her father had given her and determined to spend the lot. Surveying the results of her purchases while she sat and had a well-earned glass of iced tea, she thought that she had not done badly to make it stretch so far. She had concentrated on a few colours that she knew suited her and had managed to achieve a co-ordinated look by buying wisely and not being tempted to rash impulses.

She found herself with an array of tops, a couple of skirts, two dresses in crisp cotton, a pair of sensible shoes and a pair of lightweight sandals that were decidedly frivolous. She had renewed her underwear drawer too, discarding sensible schoolgirl things for scantily-cut bras and bikini briefs and a couple of nightdresses that were far removed from the prim, semi-Victorian ones that she usually wore.

'Shopping for your honeymoon? Your *novio* will appreciate these on your wedding night,' the shop girl who served her said with a knowing smile as she packed up the almost see-through nightdress and negligé set in shell pink that Verity had fixed upon.

'No, I'm not getting married,' she said without thinking, and then wished she hadn't when the girl gave her an even more suggestive look. Nice girls didn't anticipate the wedding in this part of the world!

Not that she could blame her, Verity thought, almost ready to say that she didn't want the items after all. Girls didn't buy that sort of lingerie for their own pleasure. It didn't belong in a virgin's bed. She wondered why she was wasting her money. She supposed it would all keep. Maybe one day she would have a husband to admire her in what she had got today. One day when she had forgotten Ramón Vance and all that he stood for and found herself a kind, caring man who loved her to distraction, faults and all. Did men like that exist? she wondered. And would she fall in love with that type even if it did?

The trouble was that a man like that would not begin to appreciate the last purchases that she made at an exclusive shop that Verity suspected Isabel patronised fairly often. The window display showed only two dresses, but one of them was sufficiently attractive for her to take her courage in both hands and ask the elderly, rather intimidating saleswoman to take it out so that she could try it on, once that she had established that it was her size.

Verity was amazed at the transformation that the mirror showed her. The schoolgirl was gone, banished for ever, and in her place was a cool, attractive young woman. The dress she had chosen was for evenings, the sort of thing that a sophisticated young woman about town might wear for soirées and cocktail parties. It was white and made from a silky material that clung, emphasising every curve of Verity's slim figure.

The *vendedora* came to the door of the changing room and nodded approvingly. '*Muy guapa, señorita,*' she said approvingly.

Verity looked at her reflection rather dubiously. 'I look different somehow,' she said aloud, wondering that a dress could make such a change in anyone.

'You look good. That dress is not for everyone, but you—you have the style to carry it off. A combination of innocence and daring, *señorita*. That is a dress to provoke a man!'

Was it? Verity wondered, and then, turning one way and then another, seeing the effect that it had as it was caught by the different shades of light, she realised that the woman was right. What would Ramón make of her, wearing a dress like this? She certainly didn't look like a child in it, she thought, as she smoothed the material over the curve of her hips and noted how trim her figure appeared.

'I'll take it,' she said, coming to a sudden decision.

And she had taken the other dress that the saleswoman had produced from a nearby rack. This one was in her favourite pink and differently styled. Less daring then the white dress, it had a certain flair to it, nevertheless, and it would be ideal if her father did carry out his intention of doing more entertaining. She could see herself as a gracious hostess, presiding over a table of guests. It was the sort of outfit that gave one confidence, she decided, although the sum total named for the two dresses nearly took her breath away.

'It will be worth it, *señorita*,' the saleswoman assured her. 'You will have pleasure wearing those dresses, and they will be much admired.'

It was to be hoped so, Verity mused as she collected her parcels together and made her way slowly back to the car. After a rapid calculation she reckoned that she probably had about five pesos left out of what her father had given her—not enough to buy even a handkerchief if she had wanted to. She put her bundles in the back of the car and settled into the driver's seat. Surprisingly, she wasn't tired, and even the prospect of the long drive home did not daunt her. If anything she felt almost exhilarated by her buying spree, sure that she had done well.

She eased out of her parking place, well pleased with herself. She had done all she had set out to do and she would be home in plenty of time. As the miles flew by she was in a fair way to thinking that the world was not a bad place, and she broke into a song as she made her journey back to Vista Hermosa. Already her mind was going ahead to the evening when she would wear her white dress to stun Ramón. He would see her as a woman then, not as a little girl. He would treat her as he treated his sophisticated girl-friends in the capital. He would admire her. He would forget Isabel, lost in admiration for the new Verity, the girl he had disregarded until now, when she blossomed forth.

It was an enjoyable daydream. So enjoyable that Verity didn't pay her usual attention to details such as the inner workings of the car. She had meant to stop for petrol just outside Córdoba. She had noticed the fuel gauge this morning as she drove in and had made a mental note to fill up the tank before she set out on the return trip. She had made sure she had left enough in her purse to pay for it. Now, when the car coughed twice and slowed down, then coughed again and coasted to a halt, she did not need to look far to discover the reason.

She was miles from anywhere, and certainly miles from the nearest petrol pump. It was too far to walk, even if she could remember in which direction the petrol station lay. She had passed one somewhere along this stretch of road, but she didn't know quite where. There was nothing to do except sit back and wait in the hope that a passing car would offer help. Verity looked at her watch and groaned. So much for a speedy journey home, she thought ruefully.

CHAPTER TEN

'WHAT's the trouble? Can we do anything for you?' A small blue Volkswagen drew to a halt beside Verity's car and the driver got out and came over to her. The other occupants of his vehicle, obviously the rest of his family, leaned out of their windows and speculated as to what was wrong.

She was lucky, really—incredibly lucky only to have been waiting for half an hour on this lonely stretch of road before someone came along. She didn't doubt that help would be forthcoming. That was the code in these parts where accidents and breakdowns were commonplace and aid was freely given by fellow travellers who knew that it might be their turn to know misfortune on their next trip.

'You wouldn't have any petrol to spare, I suppose?' she asked. Thank goodness she had attracted a family man rather than a roadside Lothario! For some men a girl on her own would be considered fair game, and she had dreaded the possibility of having to fight off someone who was over-anxious to press his attentions on her.

'Only enough to get me to the nearest *gasolinera* myself. It's about another five miles up the road. But you're welcome to a lift as far as there, if you like.'

'That would be marvellous,' Verity accepted gratefully. There seemed to be about half a dozen children packed in the car, as well as an immensely plump lady who was probably their mother. It was going to be a tight squeeze. But they made room for her obligingly after she had locked her own car carefully and joined them. In no time at all they were drawing up at a set of petrol pumps and she was able to explain her dilemma to the garage attendant.

'Can we drive you back?' Refuelled and ready for the road again, her rescuer had come over to see if she was all right.

'I'll be a while yet, thanks.' Verity indicated the search that was going on for a suitable container for her to take her petrol back to the car. She only wanted enough to get her back here in order to fill up properly, but, on his own in charge of the place, the attendant had been rather thrown by her request. He thought that he had a suitable container for her, but he wasn't sure where he had put it. 'You'd better not wait. You want to be on your way, I'm sure,' Verity said reluctantly at last.

The little man looked distressed. He wanted to help, but was equally clearly wanting to be on his way. Finally, after more lengthy protestations, he allowed himself to be persuaded and left, his family waving cheerfully to her as they drove away.

It was another hour before Verity got back to her car. She asked the garage man to drive her, but he wouldn't. '*Es impossible, señorita*,' he assured her, disappearing to answer a phone that had been ringing continuously for the last ten minutes. He was on his own here, he could not leave the *gasolinera* unattended. She would have to get a lift.

She did, and found herself driving back to her car in the cab of a long-distance truck whose driver had wandering hands. Verity was sick with relief when she managed to extract herself unmolested from his company. She sat for a few moments in her car, recovering from the experience. She was certainly sampling life today, she thought, when she finally braced herself to put her key in the ignition and drove off again.

She frowned when she was finally on her way again, the car filled with petrol and the empty container restored to the garage man. She had certainly set off in plenty of time, but now it was clear she was going to be late home. It would be dark long before she reached Vista Hermosa and she would have to slow down and drive carefully to avoid accidents. Her father might be worried about her. And Ramón would no doubt be furious, assuming that she had done it on purpose, deliberately ignoring what he had said to her.

Perhaps she should have phoned from the *gasolinera* and let them know. That would have been the best thing to do. Verity bit her lip anxiously. Why hadn't she thought of that at the time? Well, it was too late now. If there were storms ahead, she would just have to meet them head on and hope that matters weren't too bad. Surely even Ramón would be prepared to listen to a rational explanation? She would get her oar in first, explain to him what had happened. It would be all right, she thought optimistically.

When she drove carefully up the unmade track to the *estancia* and came to a halt by the house she got a fair indication of the trouble ahead of her. The front door opened, letting a blaze of light flood out on to the steps and outlining Ramón's tall figure, dark and strangely menacing as he waited there for her to get out of the car and approach him.

She could not see the expression on his face, but something about the taut stance that he took told her that he was furious. Verity shivered. It looked as if there was going to be no opportunity for reasonable excuses. She had a feeling that he wasn't in the mood for listening. For a few seconds she sat there, almost scared to stir from the driving seat. Then she pulled herself together. After all, the man couldn't eat her! She turned and collected her parcels from the back seat, then got out. She would brazen it out somehow, she resolved.

His first words to her were not exactly encouraging.

'Where the hell have you been?'

She stood on the second step up to the verandah, able now that she was near him to see the anger in his face. Somehow she did not feel like venturing any farther. 'I've been to Córdoba,' she said. 'You knew that.'

'I also knew that you were told to get back at a reasonable time.'

'You mean you ordered me to!' she flared.

'All right. So why didn't you obey orders?'

'Perhaps I didn't choose to,' she said furiously. 'I'm not obliged to. You're not my keeper, you know.' She went up the steps and stood directly in front of him now. 'Would you please let me pass?' she asked him coldly, when he showed no sign of moving aside for her. 'I'm tired and I'm fed up, and the last thing that I want at the moment is a slanging match with you on the front doorstep. Do you mind?'

'Not at all.' Ramón stood back with exaggerated politeness. 'Come in, Verity. My apologies for keeping you waiting out there.'

After she had walked past him into the hall, she heard the door slam behind her with a crash that shook the place. She had some notion of retreating to her room and locking the door, but even as she started in that direction she heard rapid steps and felt his rough grasp on her arm, seizing her in a hold that was like an iron band around her.

'I haven't finished with you yet,' he told her.

She faced him, her chin raised in defiance of him. 'I don't think there's anything that I want to say to you. So, if you'll excuse me——'

There was a white line round his mouth as if he was having trouble keeping his anger in check. It was strange that she had never seen him lose control like this before—except when he had wanted to make love to her. And she knew for a certainty that love was far from his mind at the moment.

'There's plenty I want to say to you,' he told her. 'That's if I don't give way to my first impulse, which is to twist that spoilt little neck of yours.'

'I don't have to take this sort of behaviour from you!' she raged. Impotently she wrestled with him, trying to free her wrist from his hold. 'Will you let go of me?'

'No.'

'Where's my father? Why isn't he here?' If there had been anyone else in the house the sound of two people shouting at the tops of their voices would surely have brought them running to find out what on earth was going on. It must sound as if murder was being done! Perhaps it would be before Ramón was finished with her. He was in a filthy mood.

'He's not here.'

'What do you mean? Where is he?' Verity was suddenly worried. 'Has something happened? Is he all right?'

'Oh, he's fine. It's nice of you to think about him, though,' said Ramón with heavy sarcasm. 'You callous little bitch! Why didn't you ring and let us know you were going to be late? Your father was getting anxious and I was——'

'I can imagine you shedding tears over my non-appearance,' Verity told him carelessly. 'Don't try and con me into thinking you were upset, for all that you were pacing the floor waiting for my return.'

'You'd be surprised.' His face was still dark with anger, but he seemed to be less inclined to throttle her as he had theatened. 'I've been wondering whether to ring the police or check the hospitals for you.'

She should have rung from the *gasolinera*—she acknowledged it now. Ramón and her father were right to have worried. She was over two hours later than they had expected, much later than she had imagined. Her anger died suddenly. 'I'm sorry,' she began.

'That's good to hear.' He let her go and she stood there still clutching on to her parcels.

An explanation had clearly to come now, although she felt that he would probably fly off the handle again when she admitted her stupidity. 'I ran out of petrol,' she muttered, and eyed him warily, expecting another explosion.

He ran his hand wearily through his dark hair. 'I suppose it was only to be expected. Your father wondered if that could have happened, but I told him I didn't think even you would be that stupid. It seems I was wrong.'

'Is that where Dad is? Has he gone out to meet me in the other car? Don't say I missed him somewhere on the road!'

Ramón sighed heavily, whether at her stupidity or at the fact that her father had left him to cope with it she didn't know. He glanced at his watch. 'Your father,' he said distantly, 'is by now sitting at a table at El Caballo Blanco waiting with your dinner guests for you to turn up.'

'*My* dinner guests? What are you talking about?'

'I wanted him to tell you, but he said that it would be better as a surprise. I should have insisted on letting you know. I might have known something like this

would have happened!' Ramón looked only faintly
annoyed now. Obviously it wasn't all her fault, and his
rage was no longer directed full at her. 'Your father
arranged a small celebration dinner—mainly to be a
birthday surprise for you, but partly to let people know
the good news about Vista Hermosa. We invited about
twenty people.'

'Oh!' Verity was taken aback.

'When there was no sign of you by eight o'clock I
sent your father off to greet the guests and explain that
we'd be arriving a little later. That reminds me, I'd
better ring them now and let them know we're on our
way. The restaurant's not far, we should make it by
nine-thirty if we hurry.' He moved away from her,
his hand going to the phone.

'But——'

'But what?' he asked her impatiently. 'You'd better
go and get changed, hadn't you? I assume that you're
not proposing to go dressed as you are?' His scornful
glance dismissed her pink outfit as clearly unsuitable
for the occasion.

She supposed it was. Covered in dust and rather
limp after a day in the city, it lacked the clean freshness
that it had held this morning. For the first time she
noticed that Ramón was wearing evening dress. He
looked devastatingly handsome and confident of himself in an outfit that had many men ill at ease. The
dark suit fitted his figure superbly, the white of his
silk shirt gleaming under the immaculate folds of his
black tie. No man had a right to look that sure of his
attraction for women, Verity thought. She wondered if
Isabel would be one of the party tonight. She could be
proud of her future husband.

'I'll go and get ready,' she said. 'But——' There
were questions she wanted to ask.

'Well?' His finger ready to dial the number, Ramón turned to her again.

She shook her head. 'Oh, it doesn't matter,' she said.

'Good. Now hurry up, for God's sake.'

The blazing temper had died, but it would leap to life again pretty quickly if she delayed too long over changing. She wouldn't put it past him to come to her room and help her if the mood took him. Verity washed quickly and then reached for clean underwear and tights. Automatically her hand went to the evening outfit that was hanging in her wardrobe.

And then she remembered her new dress. She sorted feverishly through the pile of parcels that she had dropped heedlessly on the floor for the one bearing the right label and, tearing aside the swathes of tissue paper in which it was encased, she pulled the dress out. She held it up against her, wondering if she had made an expensive mistake. If she had, it was too late now. Frantically she drew it over her head and let its graceful folds fall around her. She secured the zip and then studied herself in the mirror.

No, it was all right. The magic was still there, making her gasp at the picture she made. If Isabel was there tonight, she would not have her usual satisfaction at queening it over Verity. In fact she might almost be put in the shade herself. Verity applied a little make-up and a careful outline of lipstick, not too much, to give her pale, excited face a little colour. Her hair behaved for once, lying in soft waves over her shoulders, the dark chestnut highlighted by the pure white of her dress.

There—she was ready, and it had taken her only ten minutes. Even Ramón could not complain that she was slow. She thrust her feet into her new sandals and picked up her bag. On the way out of her room she could not resist another peep in the mirror—just to check that everything was all right and that her tights were not laddered, she assured herself. But it was not for that reason at all. She wanted to savour the new Verity. Her face stared back at her, her eyes darker and wider than usual and lit with an awareness that was new to them. She wasn't a scrubby little schoolgirl any more, she was a woman, and she liked the first sight of herself a good deal.

She expected Ramón to notice the difference in her when she showed herself in the hall where he was waiting, but he made no comment, merely taking her by the arm and ushering her out of the door.

'We'll be there in reasonable time after all,' he told her as he eased himself into the driving seat. 'Dinner's fixed for ten o'clock, so we'll only miss a round or so of aperitifs.'

'You haven't told me who'll be there yet. Or is that a surprise too?'

He ran through the list of names. Predictably most of them were neighbours or village folk and more her father's age group than hers, but there were a few young people that Verity knew and she liked them all. All, that was, except Isabel and her parents. She supposed that they had to be invited, it would have been rude to exclude them, but she wished with all her heart that she did not have to watch Ramón with the other girl. It cut like a knife to think of the two of them together, happy and contented, their future together settled for all time.

'Is the marriage date fixed yet, or are you still wondering if she's going to turn you down?' she asked abruptly, voicing what was in her mind.

He gave a keen look and she wondered if he thought

she was prying. 'Nothing's decided as yet,' he said briefly, and she had to be satisfied with that.

She lapsed into silence after that and he seemed quite content to share it, his gaze never once leaving the road ahead to glance in her direction. So much for her big impact on him, Verity thought dismally. Compared with the sort of women he knew, compared with Isabel even, she would always look like a dowdy provincial.

But if Ramón did not appreciate her, it was clear that other people did. When Verity entered the restaurant just in front of her escort there was an audible intake of breath, and not just from the party that was expecting her arrival. At least two of the men she passed muttered flattering comments as she passed. It was etiquette to pretend that one had not heard them, of course, but Verity felt her spirits lift all the same.

'You're here at last, love!' Her father got to his feet and embraced her. 'I was beginning to get worried about you, you know, but Vance told me there was no need. He was sure there was a rational explanation.'

So much for his tale of being on the point of ringing up hospitals! Verity gave Ramón a sideways glance, but he had not heard the remark. He was busy greeting Isabel and her parents.

She forced herself not to care. 'Car trouble, I'm afraid. Sorry if you were upset, Dad.'

'It can't be helped. Now, let me see about a drink for the birthday girl.' Mark Williams turned to find a waiter and Verity moved forward to greet everyone.

She was touched to find that most people had brought her presents—nothing wildly extravagant, but all chosen with affection and thought. Verity forced herself to think charitably even about the hideously expensive leather manicure case that Isabel pressed upon her and which she hated on sight. It was the thought that counted, she told herself firmly. It was good of the other girl to have bought her anything at all.

She looked around her with some curiosity. El Caballo Blanco was a new restaurant, which had only been going for a couple of months. Not that that made any difference to her. There were any number of eating places that were a lot older established that she had never had the opportunity to sample. At Vista Hermosa there had been neither the time nor the money for leading a giddy social life, and her convent school had offered even fewer chances.

They were taking their pre-dinner drinks in a covered courtyard which led on to the swimming pool. Apparently the place was used as a sort of country club during the day. It was possible to arrive in the morning and spend a lazy time by the pool, where waiters would serve drinks, snacks or a full lunch at tables topped by brightly covered canopies. That would be fun. Verity didn't suppose she would ever get the chance though. It didn't look like her father's sort of place, even if he took the day off, and she hardly supposed Ramón would waste time taking her out, although it was more his style.

'I'm so glad we came here,' Isabel gushed at her side. 'I've been here before, of course, but always during the day. It's quite a change to see it all lit up. The soft lighting does so much, doesn't it?'

'I suppose it does.' Verity tried to sound pleasant. After all, the other girl couldn't help what she was. After her own fashion she was probably trying to be sociable.

'You won't have been here before, of course.'

Verity's good resolutions began to fade. 'No, of course not,' she said tartly. 'We're too busy working.'

'Yes, I suppose you would be.' Isabel did not sound as if she thought much about the matter. Work was something that other people did. Her father had a ranch manager for that sort of thing and could always take time off when it suited him. 'And the subscription's quite high too.'

'I expect they don't want to lower the tone by letting the deserving poor in,' Verity said through gritted teeth. So help her, if Isabel didn't shut up pretty soon she would be finding out what it was like to sample the swimming pool fully clothed!

'You're probably right.' Isabel was bored with the topic. Once she had made her point she liked to pass on to other matters. 'Where did you get your dress?'

Other people had said it suited her, had complimented her on her choice; Isabel sounded as if she was wondering how she'd managed to afford it. 'Casa Rosada in Cordoba,' Verity said briefly, wondering how she could get away from the girl.

'Yes, I thought it looked like one of theirs. I——' Isabel broke off suddenly to slant a radiant smile over Verity's shoulder. 'Ramón!' she breathed. 'You've come to find me.'

She made his name sound like a caress. Verity flinched at the note of possession in her voice. But at least it meant that she could get away. 'Excuse me,' she said, and moved quickly away, not looking in his direction. She thought she heard him say something, but didn't look back to find out if he was talking to her. How could he be with Isabel to claim his attention? Verity chatted brightly to a young couple that she knew and convinced herself that she was having a wonderful time.

The head waiter summoned them a few minutes later with the news that their table was ready if they cared

to follow him. The dining area was very attractive with
its red-tiled floor and dark furniture. The theme of the
entire place was that of the *gaucho* and his lifestyle,
and the trappings of horsemanship were everywhere.
Silver spurs, intricately designed, hung from pillars in
the centre of the room, alongside leather harnesses and
the *boleadoras*, leather thongs attached to heavy weights
and used with incredible accuracy to fell the *gaucho*'s
prey from a distance. A mural on one wall depicted a
gaucho in traditional dress, seated on a prancing white
stallion, presumably the *caballo blanco* which the restaurant used as its name. On another was painted in
flowing characters the famous lines celebrating the
gaucho.

'And this is my pride, to live as free as the bird that
cleaves the sky,' Verity translated under her breath.
That was Ramón, she thought. It summed him up
exactly. Perhaps she should be glad that Isabel and not
herself would have the task of trying to tie him down.
She did not think it would be an easy one unless he
chose to co-operate. And he was not the sort of man to
try to compromise.

There was a lot of noise and laughter as they all
seated themselves. They had a long table and Verity
headed it with her father at the other end. Ramón, she
noticed, carefully placed himself with the Delgados.
Her attention was distracted by the waiter putting a
menu in front of her, and she concentrated on making
her choice, although she did not feel hungry. She ought
to be enjoying this, she told herself, but she knew she
wasn't. She would cry herself to sleep tonight. And
the man who made her weep would never know about
it.

Verity turned to Juan Nuñez, seated next to her and
making every effort to engage her attention. She did

not know him very well. He was a veterinary graduate, recently qualified and learning his trade by assisting old Señor Leiva in the area. He had visited Vista Hermosa many times and talked to her father.

'But I hadn't realised what a gorgeous daughter he had.' His dark eyes looked at her admiringly. 'Where's he been hiding you all this time?'

Verity laughed and responded. He was fun to talk to and he had a host of interesting stories to tell. Soon they were fast friends and he was promising to take her out with him on his trips round the countryside. 'You would like it, Verity, I'm sure. You would find it really interesting.'

'Maybe,' she responded. 'But I tend to think that every Aberdeen Angus looks pretty well the same. Are you telling me that they all have different personalities?'

'But of course they do!' He launched into the argument with enthusiasm, drawing in the people on either side, and the noise and general merriment at their end of the table became noticeable. Verity caught her father's eye and saw him grin. He was glad she was having a good time.

And she was, after a fashion, she supposed. She glanced at her watch and was quite surprised to see how the time was slipping by. The food was delicious and she managed to eat more of it than she had expected. The flattering way that the men were eyeing her was a boost to her damaged ego. Ramón Vance might not appreciate her charms, but other men did, she consoled herself.

She looked up the table to see if he had noticed the amount of attention that she was getting—and then wished that she hadn't. He was staring straight at her and his expression was grim. What was the matter with him? Couldn't she enjoy her birthday dinner without him glowering at her? What had she done now to offend him? Or was he just recalling the events of earlier in the evening and remembering that her lateness could have deprived him of precious time in Isabel's company? She was sure that was why he had been so cross with her when she had finally got home. Ramón Vance was not accustomed to waiting around for one woman when he wanted to be with another. Verity wondered why he had sent her father on ahead instead of coming to greet their guests himself.

She could not make him out. He had looked at her just now as if he could kill her, but the next second she saw his sleek dark head bent in Isabel's direction, saying something that the other girl obviously found amusing, for she was smiling up at him in a high good humour.

Juan was saying something to her, but suddenly Verity didn't want to listen any more. Why should she try and fool herself that boys like him could ever mean anything to her? Juan had made it very clear that he was interested in her. If she cared to encourage him, he was good husband material. And, even if it did not go as far as that, he would be an entertaining escort until the time came for her to leave Vista Hermosa.

But she could not use people like that. It would be what Isabel would do in her situation, she was sure. The other girl would not be averse to playing one man off against another, bettering her own position all the time. She must have been born with the ability to handle men, Verity thought. It was something you either had or you did without. You couldn't learn it, however hard you tried.

Her head ached and she longed to get away for a few minutes. No one would miss her if she slipped out for a breath of air. They would assume she had gone to the cloakroom. Verity muttered a quick word of excuse and left the table.

Outside the night air was cool against her face and she breathed deeply, savouring the relief it brought her. She had come through the courtyard where they had been earlier and stood by the edge of the pool. The water slapped against the tiled sides with a small swirling sound that was very restful after the uproar that she had just left. She bent down and dabbled her hand in the water, revelling in the coolness. She wished she did not have to go back to the party.

She did not hear a step behind her and started violently when a voice asked, 'Planning a dip? I wouldn't advise it in that dress.'

Why did it have to be him of all people? Why had he chosen to follow her out? Verity did not reply. Perhaps he would get the message and leave her alone.

But it seemed that Ramón, usually so aware of her thoughts, failed to read them with his customary accuracy. Either that or he was ignoring the signals that she was putting out. 'I wanted to be alone,' she said pointedly.

'Waiting for young Nuñez to join you for a romantic assignation? There doesn't seem to be any moonlight, but I don't imagine you'll miss it.' His voice sounded harsh and critical.

'And if I was?' she asked him.

'You'd be a fool. He's not for you, for all your determined flirting with him over the dinner table.'

So he *had* been watching her. She did not know what to make of that. She shrugged. 'A girl can't behave like a nun all the time.'

'I don't think there's any danger of that,' he told her.

She was silent, thinking of the ample proof that she had given him of exactly how wanton she could be. Did he think she was like that with every man she met, that she responded as uninhibitedly as she had done with him? She never knew what he thought. That was half her trouble.

'I see you're wearing my present,' he said.

Verity's hand went up to clutch the small silver thistle that lay at her breast. She had picked it up from the table and had taken it to her room before she had set out for Córdoba that morning. She had weakened and tried it on and had then been reluctant to take it off. She had worn it because she loved it and because Ramón had given it to her. And, because her pink dress had a high neck that hid the pendant from view, she had gone out wearing it, secure in the knowledge that if she bumped into him on the way to the car he would not be able to tell that she had it on.

Tonight, when she had changed, she had forgotten about it until the last minute and then it had been too late to take it off. And she had not wanted to. She had not thought he would notice. He had been too angry with her to bother about details like that.

'This dress has a low neck. It needed something, and I don't have any other jewellery,' she made rapid excuses. She played nervously with it, wishing he would drop the subject.

'Don't fiddle with it, you'll break it.' There was an edge to his voice.

'You make me nervous,' she muttered.

'Do I, Verity?'

'You always have.'

He was close enough to touch her now, but he didn't. She knew she wanted him to, and she was ashamed of the tide of feeling that swept over her as she caught the remembered scent of his cologne.

'I wonder why that should be?' he asked her.

'I don't know,' she spoke in a tight little voice that didn't seem to belong to her. She must sound impossibly naïve. She moved agitatedly to one side in an effort to get away from him, but caught her heel in her dress and stumbled. She would have fallen in the water if he had not moved to catch her. 'I'm sorry.' She missed a breath as his arms came round her. 'I'm stupid.'

'You're impossible.' He pulled her up against him. 'What am I going to do with you, Verity?'

She raised her face in mute invitation. She could not help herself. For a long moment Ramón studied her, and then he kissed her, hungrily, as if he could not hold back any longer.

When he raised his head from hers she muttered a protest and he claimed her lips again. 'Oh God, but I want you, Verity,' he groaned.

'I want you too,' she whispered.

'And that's all it is between us, do you think?' he asked her. 'There's nothing more?'

There was everything more. From her side, at least. Was that what he wanted, the satisfaction of knowing he had captured the best prize of all? Did he want to hear her say that she loved him? Verity was past evasions now, past all caring. He wanted her and he would take her. And for a while it would be bliss. And that happy time would make up for the misery that followed. That was inevitable.

'I love you,' she said. Just the simple truth.

'Verity?' He sounded amazed.

'I know that it's Isabel that you want to marry. But you *want* me, don't you?'

'Ever since the first day I met you.' His voice

sounded ragged. 'But about Isabel——'

'I mind—I'd be a fool if I didn't. But I'll accept it. I'll be your mistress until you marry her. Afterwards—I'll go away somewhere. I couldn't bear it, if——'

'Little fool,' he said, but he was suddenly tender. 'Verity, my poor love, you don't have to bear anything ever again. I'll be around to look after you in the future—or at least to try.' He smiled down at her. 'That prickly independence of yours will take a bit of a knock, I'm afraid.'

'But you're going to marry Isabel.'

'I'm going to marry you. If you'll have me.'

'But you've been going around with her for weeks now. And you told me you were getting married,' she accused him.

'I don't remember telling you the lady's name. You just jumped to conclusions the way you usually do, my love. And I admit I fully intended you to.'

'You're playing games with me, Ramón!'

'Yes,' he admitted. 'I deliberately set out to make you jealous. You told me so vehemently that I meant nothing to you, yet every time I laid a finger on you, you responded in a very satisfactory way. I told you I didn't play fair, Verity. When it's a question of getting what I want I go all out for it.'

'But you were so angry with me tonight when I got home. I thought you were cross because I'd kept you away from Isabel——'

'I was half out of my mind with worry about you,' he said, frowning at the memory. 'When you were a little late I told myself that you were just trying to show who was boss, but when time went on and you still hadn't appeared I changed my tune. I was thinking of road accidents and the lot. I've never been so scared in my life.'

'Scared? You?' Verity asked incredulously. 'I can't imagine it.'

'And you can't believe I could love you either, can you? Have I treated you so badly?'

'Yes,' she said baldly. 'And I'm going to take a bit of convincing.'

'I'll do my best to tell you, darling.' And his mouth covered hers again.

Long moments later Verity asked, 'Won't Isabel be very disappointed that you're not going to marry her?'

'Probably. But since I never asked her she can't really complain. She had her hopes, I suppose. But she'll get over it in time,' Ramón said carelessly.

From indoors came the sound of cheers and clapping.

'They're drinking toasts,' he said. 'They missed you. Young Nuñez was coming out to find you, but I sent him back and came myself.'

'Jealous?' she asked, amazed.

'Very. And don't tell me I had no need to be—I saw you flirting with him all through dinner.' He looked down at her. 'If we went in now we could give them something else to drink to,' he said persuasively.

'I haven't said that I'll marry you yet.' Verity paused, thinking aloud. 'You realise that it'll wreak havoc with my education? I was going to England to study.'

'You could get your degree here in Argentina. We'll travel to England, I promise you. I'll take you anywhere you want to see. But I'm not letting you disappear for three years just when I've found you.'

'We'll talk about it later. It's all too sudden at the moment. Two hours ago I didn't even like you,' she said.

'And now?'

She studied his dark features. 'Now I'm not sure.'

'You'll have a lifetime to find out.'

'Will that be long enough?' she teased him.

'I might just tame you by the time you're an old lady with your grandchildren at your knee. Perhaps. But *I'm* looking forward to the challenge. Can't you do likewise?'

'We'll fight,' she warned him.

'Like cat and dog,' he agreed. 'Scared, Verity?'

She shook her head.

'I'll make you happy, I promise you that. You won't regret it in the end.'

'You're always so sure of yourself, aren't you?' she sighed ruefully.

'In this case I think I can afford to be. Can't I?' he asked her, pulling her closer to him.

'Probably,' she agreed. Ramón would have his own way. He always did. But the prospect didn't worry her. In this case at least she had a feeling that he was right. She smiled up at him. 'Let's go and break the news,' she said softly.

And they went in together.

We value your opinion...

You can help us make our books even better by completing and mailing this questionnaire. Please check [✓] the appropriate boxes.

1. Compared to romance series by other publishers, do Harlequin novels have any additional features that make them more attractive?

   1.1 ☐ yes   .2 ☐ no   .3 ☐ don't know

   If yes, what additional features? _____

   _____

   _____

2. How much do these additional features influence your purchasing of Harlequin novels?

   2.1 ☐ a great deal   .2 ☐ somewhat   .3 ☐ not at all   .4 ☐ not sure

3. Are there any other additional features you would like to include?

   _____

   _____

   _____

4. Where did you obtain this book?

   4.1 ☐ bookstore   .4 ☐ borrowed or traded

   .2 ☐ supermarket   .5 ☐ subscription

   .3 ☐ other store   .6 ☐ other (please specify)_____

5. How long have you been reading Harlequin novels?

   5.1 ☐ less than 3 months   .4 ☐ 1-3 years

   .2 ☐ 3-6 months   .5 ☐ more than 3 years

   .3 ☐ 7-11 months   .6 ☐ don't remember

6. Please indicate your age group.

   6.1 ☐ younger than 18   .3 ☐ 25-34   .5 ☐ 50 or older

   .2 ☐ 18-24   .4 ☐ 35-49

Please mail to: **Harlequin Reader Service**

In U.S.A.	In Canada
1440 South Priest Drive	649 Ontario Street
Tempe, AZ 85281	Stratford, Ontario N5A 6W2

Thank you very much for your cooperation.

FREE!
Romance Treasury

A beautifully bound, value-packed, three-in-one volume of romance!

Romance Treasury

An exciting opportunity to collect treasured works of romance! Almost 600 pages of exciting romance reading in each beautifully bound hardcover volume!

You may cancel your subscription whenever you wish! You don't have to buy any minimum number of volumes. Whenever you decide to stop your subscription just drop us a line and we'll cancel all further shipments.